ELIZABETH AND THE CLAN OF DRAGONS

A REVERSE HAREM PARANORMAL ROMANCE

AVA MASON

For Raven

1

*I*f I didn't have wolf eyesight, I wouldn't have been able to see the form of the two wolves creeping towards our house. One of them had long beautiful golden-red fur, the kind you just wanted to run your fingers through. But, not once did I reach out even just for a simple caress. I didn't dare. This was the wolf who wanted to kill me.

I took a sip from my delicate porcelain teacup and blanched as it went down my throat; it was now tepid. My eyes followed them as they crept closer to the house and I was tempted to call for my father, the Alpha of our pack, but I held off, waiting to see what they would do.

The second wolf had golden fur, without any reddish tint, and suddenly he sat on his hind legs and looked up at me. I froze in place, my hand grasping the handle of my cup, wondering if he could see me.

I was on the top floor of the house in a wide open white room, staring through the wall of glass into the dark forest below. Even though my room was dark, I lived in a glass palace. If any moonlight shone through the windows at all, then for sure he knew I was watching him. I stuck my tongue out at him and his head rolled to the side, considering me. I waited in tight anticipation for his reaction.

I'd known Aaron since I was a baby pup; he'd been born just one full moon after me. This caused considerable consternation to his father because, as the oldest pup in the pack, I was destined to be the future Alpha.

Yep, that's right. The moon chose me. Fated Alpha of the whole friggin pack.

And it must seriously be having an outright belly laugh because the problem was, I couldn't shift.

&

I CONSIDERED TAKING MY CLOTHES OFF JUST TO PISS AARON OFF because he still hadn't moved. Of course, shifter wolves were used to being naked around each other. But Aaron still got flustered when I was naked around the pack because I never had a reason to be. Naked that is. On account of my not being able to shift and all that shit. And he *really* hated it when I undressed in front of my windows.

I jumped out of my skin as light flooded my room. "Elizabeth."

"What the he—" I stopped myself in time to cut off the mid-level curse that formed on my lips. My dad was very strict: no cussing in the house. Or in the car. And especially not in church.

That just meant that I cursed like a sailor whenever I could, as long as he wasn't around.

I turned towards my dad, taking note that while I was busy spilling tea on my shirt, Aaron had slipped out of sight. Coward. I would razz him about it later. That's if he would let me.

I faced my father, smiling and really grateful that I hadn't giving Aaron a strip show. "Hey, you scared me."

He didn't answer but stared at me, frowning, and I wondered if I had chocolate on my face or something. I tried to wipe at my mouth inconspicuously but of course, my dad noticed. He noticed everything.

Finally, he spoke. "Have you been sneaking into the chocolate?"

I shook my head. "Of course not."

"Then why can I smell it from here?"

Damn it. Of course he could smell it. "Not in the past hour, I haven't."

The lines on his forehead deepened and his blue eyes pierced into mine. "You know that's for tomorrow."

"But if it's for *my* party, then why can't I taste it a little? Just to make sure that I'll like it."

His hand whipped forward and before I could stop him, he'd reached into the front pocket of my jacket and pulled out a handful of wrappers. He held it to my face. "A little?"

He couldn't help the smile that had begun to snake up his lips, so he pressed them into a thin line.

"I brought those from home. My home." Just one lie after the other, they sure knew how to roll right off my lips without thinking about it. And that was usually the problem. I didn't think about my lies before I told them and that's what always got me into trouble. Thank goodness they were almost always white lies, so obvious that everyone knew that they were lies.

Except the one about Aaron.

No one knew about that. And no one must ever know.

My dad sighed, rubbing his face. "Elizabeth."

"Scarface is here." I blurted this out, trying to direct his attention from the lecture he most certainly was about to give me.

"Of course he's here. I asked him to come. And stop calling him that."

I'd dubbed Aaron's dad, Scarface. Everyone in the pack knew it and I'd even heard other people say it, much to my absolute giddiness, but no one ever called him that to his face. Most especially not me.

You know, because of the whole 'he wants to kill me' thing.

People thought it was because of the long scar that ran from his eye to the bottom of his jaw but the real reason I called him that was because I knew deep inside that he would really kill me if he ever had the chance, just like Scar killed his King in Lion King.

"I asked Garrett and Aaron to come so we could talk about

tomorrow." My dad looked over my clothes - I was wearing sweat-pants and a tank top under my jacket. His face was serious again, and I felt the weight of the pack slowly begin to descend on my shoulders.

Tomorrow was my birthday. We were going to have a humongous celebration, followed by a meeting of the pack council. All of the leaders were going to vote on whether or not they would pick a new Fated Alpha if I didn't come into my shifter powers by the time I was twenty-five: only one year and two hours away.

You couldn't have an Alpha who couldn't even shift.

It was ridiculous some said and I agreed wholeheartedly. Unfortunately, my dad didn't. He trusted that my shifter powers would come eventually. That I was a late bloomer, just like my mother.

Well, thanks mom, for giving me latent wolf powers.

"I'm asking Garrett to vote against assigning a new leader."

I raised my eyebrows. "Dad, you know Scarface hates me. He won't help you. In fact, he'll probably lobby to move Aaron up now, seeing how he's the strongest of all the pups."

"You don't know that. I believe he'll help. Get dressed, I want you in on the meeting." He walked toward my door. "And for heaven's sake, switch the tint so no one can see you."

Yes, my dad is as honorable and as naive as they come. He thinks people are just as principled as he is. But he would be wrong about Garrett. I knew it. I just had to find a way to prove it.

I pushed the magical button on the wall that switched the tint from 'day' to 'night.' Okay not *really* magical but it was science and math or something, so it was magical to me. It allowed you to see outside while at the same time no one could see you. But you had to push the button after the sun went down because the settings were different. I sighed, wishing that I had automatic ones like in my parents' room.

I peaked through the window one more time to see if Aaron was still there. If so, I may turn the blinders back to 'day' while I undressed just to piss him off but there was no sign of him.

I turned back to my childhood room, disappointed, and went to the pile of dirty clothes on the dark hardwood floor to pull out something to wear. No use smelling fresh for their arrival.

I didn't live here anymore, I had my own home closer to the city, thank heavens, but I was still here often enough to have a pile of dirty clothes. Even though I'd grown up in this room, my mom redecorated the minute I moved out. Gone were the bright colors and fan-girl posters of my youth, replaced by white walls, delicate white duvets, and silver furniture. I think she was so sick of the mess and colors, that she just made everything white to get rid of her headache.

But still, I liked it. There was a simple elegance to it.

I rummaged through the pile of dirty clothes and found the flannel shirt and pair of jeans that I'd worn while out a while ago. I shrugged into them, taking a deep breath to revel in the smell of dirt and dead leaves.

I wanted to be as dirty and smelly as possible to annoy Scarface without pissing off my dad.

I grinned, thinking about how Aaron also liked me dirty.

۶★

WHEN AARON SAW ME, HE JUMPED TO HIS FEET, EYES WIDE, AND HIS face a scowl. Then he bent over, bowing. His father was slower, his chair scraped hesitatingly across the hardwood floor until he finally stood up to bow. I scampered to my seat and as soon as I was in it, they sat back down.

As Fated Alpha of the pack, it was a sign of respect to bow when I entered the room during a meeting. Honestly, it made me uncomfortable and was sometimes downright annoying but it was pack formality and all that. You had to pick your battles. Besides, it was better than how they acted when my dad walked in. I was just glad that my dad was already in the room.

As soon as we were settled in at the long walnut conference table, my dad began the meeting with the most boring topic ever: insurance coverage for the families in the pack.

Apparently, he didn't want to get straight to the point. Maybe he thought that if he bored Scarface to death, Scarface would give in to my dad's demands, just to get him to shut up. I imagined him standing up and screaming. "I'll vote against a new Alpha. I'll give you all my money. I'll do whatever you want. Just no more meetings about insurance!"

I stifled a laugh but it came out like a snort and suddenly all eyes were on me. I started fake coughing to try to cover up my gaff.

Aaron shot out of his seat and his leather chair almost fell to the floor. "I think she needs water, I'll take her to get some."

I raised my eyebrow at him and he gave me an urgent look. What was his deal? I played along anyway, coughing louder and Aaron pounded on my back. "She must have something in her throat." He took my arm. "Come on, let's get you some water."

Scarface rolled his eyes while my dad searched my hands for what I assumed was chocolate candy wrappings or something of the sort. In any event, we really weren't fooling them but they didn't say anything as we walked out of the conference room.

❧

WE WALKED DOWN THE HALLWAY AND I PRESSED MY HAND TO THE wallpaper dotted with silver palm leaves, feeling the bumps as I walked. As soon as we were out of hearing distance, Aaron grabbed my arm and shoved me into the guest bathroom.

I yelped, surprised, and he shut the door quietly behind him and then turned to me.

"Are you crazy?" He whispered in an angry voice. "Why did you have to wear those clothes? My dad might smell me on them. And how long has it been since you've done your laundry?"

I waved my hand, dismissing him. "He won't. If he smells anything, it's that bad cologne you're wearing." I giggled and he put his finger to my mouth, warning me to be quiet. That was a lie, his cologne was intoxicating.

Putting my hand on his to hold it still, I opened my mouth and slipped his finger between my lips. He froze as I sucked it in deeper while rolling my tongue around it. He made a small guttural noise and I began to pull up his shirt.

He yanked his finger out of my mouth to stop me from pulling his shirt. "Lizzy, we can't. Not right now, they'll come looking for us."

I leaned forward, pressing my breasts against his chest and grinned. "We'd better hurry then." I placed my hand under his shirt and his skin heated at my touch. I caressed his stomach with my fingertips. "They won't come for a while because my dad is working his way up to asking your dad to vote 'no' tomorrow."

He raised his eyebrows. "Are you serious?"

I nodded, then moved my hand lower, feeling him harden through his pants. I tried to pull his shirt off him again but he still held it tight, his face looking over my shoulder into the mirror as he thought about what I'd just told him.

Giving up on him, I began to unbutton my own shirt instead. "Remember the button that used to be here?" I pointed to the empty spot where my top button used to be and he looked down. "Remember how I lost that?"

His cheeks tinged pink, remembering that in his passion he'd popped the button off impatiently. He made a breathy noise as he watched me slowly reveal myself to him, inch by inch as my buttons came undone. When I was done, I opened my shirt and let it fall to the floor.

He gasped, reaching to stroke the tops of my shoulder and I lowered his hand to my breast. He took a deep breath in, remembering our romp in the woods, I'm sure.

Sighing, he leaned his head on mine, stroking me through the thin lace of my bra and my nipple hardened.

A warm glow washed through my body; every nerve in my body called for him. I was strung so tight and needed the release that only he could give me.

"Aaron, please. I need you. I'm worried about tomorrow." This wasn't one of my white lies.

In times past, I wouldn't have had to beg. But things were changing and now he wasn't always willing to play along with my antics.

Sometimes he could even be quite moody about it.

He hesitated and I knew I had him where I wanted him. "Please? As a birthday gift?"

He groaned, giving in, and then whipped his shirt off. I eyed him hungrily, taking in the muscles of his chest. Unable to stop myself, I moved my hands over them, loving the feel of his tight ridges. His hand moved back to my neck, splaying his fingers across it, then he leaned forward and began to kiss my shoulder.

His lips felt like flames licking my skin and my mouth fell open as they traveled to my neck and suckled the sensitive spot at the base of my throat. I pressed my hands into his back, loving the way his muscles grew taught at my touch. Then I moved them back around to the front of his chest, touching, feeling, needing. Anywhere I could touch, I touched. Anywhere I could feel, I felt. His smell, light and woodsy, wrapped around me, drawing me deeper into his touch.

His lips moved with urgency as they traveled up my throat and then his lips met mine. His mouth was hot and possessive and his tongue pushed my lips open. I sucked his tongue in greedily, pulling him closer. I needed to feel every inch of his naked body on me.

Growling, he lowered his hands to my ass and squeezed it, then yanked me off the floor and sat me on the bathroom counter. I opened my legs so he could stand between them, and then wrapped them around his waist, drawing him in even closer.

Even though I tried not to show it, I was worried about letting down my family and my pack every day. And every day that drew closer to my next birthday felt like a betrayal to them, to my breed. But Aaron was my grounding. His touch sent a warmth through my body, calming me in a way that he would never understand. I needed him in my life.

As his lips devoured mine, his hand caressed my shoulder again and then he gently pulled my bra strap down. I yanked the other one down, eager for his mouth on me. His lips trailed down my collar and he pulled the cup of my bra down, exposing my breast. His mouth closed over it, suckling it softly, then nimbly flicked the tip with his tongue.

I gasped, throwing my head back as the sensation in my body built up, making me lose all control. I grasped at the front of his pants, rubbing up and down and he paused for a second to revel in my touch.

Then he pulled me off the counter and tore the middle of my bra apart and dropped it to the floor. Kneeling down, he gripped my breasts in his hands and squeezed them together, licking and biting them.

A burning began low in my belly and whimpering noises escaped my mouth. My need and want and desire rolled through my body, lighting me on fire. He flicked my nipples with his thumb and little bursts of electricity shot down into the lower part of my body. I began to rub myself against him, needing the release.

"Please." My voice came out desperate. "I need you inside me."

He growled, popped open the button on my jeans and yanked them down. Then he crouched down, tracing his tongue up my inner thigh until it was on my sensitive spot, teasing me through the thin material. I whimpered as he slipped his finger past the lace. I arched my back, ready to explode at the slightest touch.

"Elizabeth?" My father's voice was down the hall.

We both froze, staring into each other's eyes like deer in headlights. The spell was broken and we scrambled to help each other get dressed. If we were caught, his father would kill him and my status as the future pack alpha would be in serious jeopardy. I wasn't allowed to pick a mate until I could shift and sexual relationships with other potential alphas was strictly forbidden.

Not that I really cared about that.

While I pulled my pants up, he picked my bra up off the ground. I grabbed it out of his hands and, instead of putting it on, I shoved it in my pocket. I was pretty sure he'd broken it anyway. He was buttoning up my shirt and I was searching the floor for his. Spotting it, I leaned over, picked it up and then yanked it over his head.

For a moment, his hands were stuck over his head and I stifled a laugh. Finally, he pulled it down and then he looked down with a frown. "It's on backwards."

"Shoot!" I yanked it back over his chest, twisted it so that it was the right way and then pulled it back down again.

We were dressed in five seconds and I turned around to face the mirror. I could still feel his hardness behind me and for a moment, I closed my eyes and pressed back into him.

He groaned, clinging to the edge of the marble counter.

Dammitall to hell. The stupid rules.

He leaned forward, pushing me with him and turned the water on. His lips pressed against my ear and his breath gave me goosebumps. "Later."

He opened the drawer and pulled out one of the paper cups we used when the guests brushed their teeth.

I nodded, flashing him a grin in the mirror as I took it from him. I filled it up and then gulped it down. I needed to cool down, especially if my dad were to find us. He'd probably smell our pheromones a mile away.

Aaron dropped to the tiled floor and counted while he did twenty rapid fire pushups, using the exercise to push the blood through his body. When he stood up, I handed him the cup and he put it to his lips, meeting my eyes as he drank the cool water. Opening the cabinet door, I squatted down and reached to the back, where I hid his cologne. It was the good kind; strong enough to mask his pheromones. I sprayed it over him lightly as he crushed the paper cup in his hands and, handing it to me, left the bathroom.

☙

I STARED AT MY REFLECTION IN THE MIRROR FOR A MOMENT, GIVING Aaron time to return to the conference room before me. My face was flushed, my lips swollen and even I could sense my own need. I splashed water over my face and ran my fingers through my hair, then squirted my own body spray in the essential places.

If my father said anything about my long absence, I could claim not feeling well; I did eat a lot of candy after all. I smirked at my reflection and then left the bathroom.

As soon as I closed the bathroom door behind me, the silhouette of my dad's large frame filled the end of the hallway. I immediately knew he was furious; I'd been gone too long. I met him in the hallway, my hand on my stomach. He didn't say a word but I followed him, my symbolic tail between my legs, to the conference room.

Just as we reached it, Scarface was leaving with Aaron trailing behind him. Scarface sneered at my father. "If she can't be bothered to be in her own meeting, then I don't see a reason why I should care about her position as the Fated Alpha."

My father put his hand on Scarface's shoulder, attempting to placate him. "She was in the bathroom, Garrett. You can't expect her to—"

"I expect her to act like a responsible adult and show some concern for the pack. If she really cared about the future of the pack, she would have come into her shifter powers by now."

Scarface always talked about me, around me and at me, but never *to* me. Now he talked about me like I wasn't even in the room.

"Honestly," he continued, "I didn't want to have to tell you this but I don't even think that she could lead the pack if she ever came into her powers." He turned to me now, giving me a contemptuous look as he brushed past me. "She's weak and unfit to rule the pack. We'll finish this business tomorrow evening."

Then he was gone and Aaron, red faced and submissive to his dominating father, left with him and the silence in the room was deafening.

As he'd spoken those horrible words I'd held in my tears. That was another rule but it wasn't just one of my father's rules. It was pack rule, and law of the jungle. Never show weakness.

Now they fell down my face but I hastily wiped them away, not even wanting my father to see them. My face was flushed a bright red and I couldn't look at my father.

He sighed and slumped into one of the chairs, then ran his hands through his hair.

I stood, frozen and unsure what to do. And then I sat on the floor at his feet and leaned my head against his legs. "I'm sorry, Dad."

He put his hand on top of my head and rubbed it softly, the bottom of his silver onyx ring scratching my head.

"He's right, Dad. I am the weakest member of this pack. Even if I—"

He interrupted me. "When. Even *when* you develop your wolf powers."

I sighed, frustrated. "What if I don't though, Dad? And even if I do, all the other wolves are light years ahead of me. I'll never be as strong or as smart as them. How will I ever know how to lead them?" The doubt had lingered in my mind, a dark cloud over my head everywhere I went but I'd never spoken the words out loud to him, until now. "They should find another leader, one better to lead the pack."

His legs shuffled and I sat back, then he eased out of his chair to sit next to me on the floor. I lowered my head, unworthy to be on the same level as him. He pulled up my chin so that I could meet him in the eyes.

"Always look someone in the eyes when you apologize, even if you are not their equal."

I blinked, afraid to look him in the eyes but even more afraid now to look down. "I'm sorry, Dad. Can you forgive me? I was stupid and worried."

"What were you doing for so long?"

"My stomach ached." I spoke this lie with conviction for it had to be convincing. He could never know the truth about Aaron.

He raised his eyebrow and then reached into his pocket and pulled out a piece of chocolate. I eyed it warily; I really had eaten way too many earlier.

He unwrapped it and put it into his mouth with one large bite. "I told you, you shouldn't have eaten the candy. I put a magical spell on it to make you sick if you snuck into them."

I grinned at his lie and relief washed over me. He wasn't mad at me.

"So what are you going to—"

"Hush, dear." He pulled on my hand so that I twisted around to sit in his lap. I couldn't remember the last time I'd sat here; it must've been at least fourteen years or more. Even though I was older now, I still felt very small next to him.

"We'll worry about that later. Garrett just needed an excuse to deny my request."

I straightened and turned to face him in shock. "So you do believe me."

"Of course. I know he doesn't want you to be Alpha. Anyone with eyes and half a brain could see that. But that doesn't mean that you let on that you know."

I mulled this thought over.

"When you become Alpha, always keep your friends close and your enemies closer. And never let them know that they are your enemy until you are ready to play your hand." His eyes bore into mine. "And never play your hand until you know you will win. I knew tonight that he would find an excuse to turn me down and so I forced him to play his hand. Tomorrow, he will see mine."

My eyes widened. "What are you going to do?"

He shook his head. "It's late and you need to go to bed."

"Dad, I'm too old for a bed time."

"I know, but I have things I need to do to finish preparing for tomorrow. And you need your beauty rest. Your mother will kill me if you aren't perfect for tomorrow." He hesitated and I knew there was something he wanted to tell me. He put his hands on my shoulder. "Don't worry about anything tomorrow. Just enjoy being young and single and having a birthday."

"But we haven't celebrated my birthday like this in a few years."

"I know, but your mom and I decided to throw you one last big one. We have a feeling it's going to be a special one." He paused for a moment. "I've been waiting to train you how to be a leader because it's much easier when you have your dormant Alpha powers. But I see now that I made the wrong choice. I will begin to train you after your birthday, powers or not."

I nodded in agreement and stood up, growing sleepy. He stood up with me and kissed me goodnight on my forehead. Just as I was about to leave, he stopped me.

"Elizabeth, your mother was twenty-seven when she got her wolf powers."

"I know, you both told me a zillion times."

"What we didn't tell you is that your mom's powers came to her immediately, without any training. Sometimes, dear daughter, we just *are*."

I raised my eyebrows, puzzled at this new information. I opened my mouth to ask him more but he shooed me with his hand, motioning for me to go to bed. Regretfully, I turned towards my room to let him work.

❧

AS I PADDED TOWARDS MY ROOM, I SLIPPED MY PHONE OUT OF MY pocket. I had a text from Aaron.

Sorry.

My thumb flew over my keyboard to text a response. *All my fault.*

After a moment, my phone dinged with a response.

My dad's pissed. Yours?

I typed back. *No. Just...* I took a moment to think about it. *Disappointed.*

Ugh. That's worse. Especially coming from your dad.

I know.

The phone was silent for a while and I almost thought he'd gone to bed. I went back to my room and began to unbutton my shirt. In the middle of my shirt, I noticed one of my buttons was off and I froze, my hands tight on my shirt.

Had my dad noticed?

I mulled it over, going over everything my dad did from the time I left the bathroom to the time I came to my room. I couldn't think of anything amiss. No strange looks or staring at my shirt for a moment too long so I dismissed the thought.

After putting on my sweats, I went to my closet to stare at the dress I would wear tomorrow. It was a golden color that brought out

14

my tan, and was lined with satin. I moved my hand down it. Aaron would die when he saw me in it.

At this thought my phone pinged again. *Look out your window.*

I rushed to the window and Aaron stepped out from behind a large tree, naked.

What are you doing here?

I told you 'later'.

But what about your Dad? He'll kill you if he finds you missing.

He's gone; he won't be home until late.

How do you know?

Because he's done it every single night this week.

He has? This information worried me. Maybe my dad didn't know everything.

Are you coming?

I stared out the window, biting my lip. I knew that he couldn't see me.

I typed my response. *Hold up, I'll be there in a sec.* Then I threw my phone on my bed and quietly moved down the hall and paused at my dad's office door. His voice murmured; he was talking on the phone but I couldn't understand what he was saying. He'd soundproofed the room.

Well, as much as you could soundproof a room from wolf ears.

His voice was commanding, but urgent. Maybe he did know what Scarface was up to.

I moved away from his office and towards the back door, grateful that my mom was already asleep.

I was afraid of my dad but I was even more afraid of my mom. If she knew I wasn't getting my beauty rest the night before my big party, she would tan my ass.

Noting that the alarm hadn't been turned on yet, I opened the back door and slipped out into the cool night.

2

*A*s soon as I was within the trees, he stepped out and yanked me towards him. His mouth was on mine, possessive and needy, and my whole body felt like it was on fire. I pushed him back into the cover of the trees and he yanked my shirt off, this time popping all my buttons off.

He threw my shirt to the ground and was already pulling my sweats down. I bent my knees, helping him slide them off and then he pushed me against a tree, a low growl in his throat.

I stood on my tiptoes, reaching up to kiss him and I heard the crinkle of the condom package. I put my arms around his neck and nipped his shoulder while he wrapped himself.

Then he grabbed my ass and pulled me up to press against the tree. I pulled aside my panties to guide him inside. Panty-wearing sex felt sexier sometimes.

His face was pure ecstasy as he entered me and I moved my hips to encourage him. My nipples prickled with the cold even though my whole body was on fire. I arched my back and teased my nipples with my fingers, putting on a show.

He moaned. "Fuck, Elizabeth. You are so gorgeous."

His need drove him now and my back scratched against the rough bark of the tree as he pumped in and out but I didn't care. I licked my fingers, then put them back on my nipples, flicking them. He groaned in response, too overcome by his need to say anything.

Damn, he felt so good inside me. I lowered one of my hands to stroke my clit and my whole body roared in response. The pressure began to build as tingling sensations shot through me. His mouth was open and I knew that he was close.

I rubbed harder, pressing on the perfect spot as he filled me, wanting to come the same time as him. Then he called out my name, his voice a gravelly groan. With the sound of my name on his lips, I exploded as my orgasm rushed through my veins, sending waves of pleasure through my body.

He grinned with satisfaction and I met his smile with my own. Then he leaned his head on my shoulder.

"I'm sorry."

I frowned. "For what?"

"I didn't please you first. That was selfish of me."

I pulled my head back to look at him. "That's okay, I know how to please myself if necessary."

His lips twisted in a half grin.

"Besides, you can make it up to me tomorrow."

His eyebrows furrowed. "Tomorrow?"

I shrugged. "Yeah, tomorrow."

"We're not going to sneak off tomorrow. Things are bad enough as they are. You're not worried about what's going to happen?"

My body slid down his, slippery from my desire and I fixed my underwear. "It doesn't really matter. I don't think I'm meant to be the Alpha." My hand flew to my mouth; the words that played over and over in my mind had slipped from my lips.

"What?" His voice was incredulous. "Is that what your dad told you?"

"No." I bit my lip, looking away and Aaron's hand was on my shoulder, trying to comfort me. My defenses were down when I was with Aaron, his concern for me made me feel like I could show my true self.

"What if..." I looked him in the eyes and decided to be brave. "What if I agree with your dad? What if you're what's best for the pack?"

"That's not true." The conviction in his eyes made me believe him, yet the fact that he didn't judge me made me feel even worse. I was weak.

"Elizabeth." He leaned his forehead on mine as his words wrapped around my body, warming the small space in my chest reserved for the one true mate who would belong to me. "I believe in you. Don't doubt yourself." He frowned, even as his fingers found my breast and he played with the tips of them while he considered my words. I leaned in closer, stifling my moan. He didn't even realize what he was doing to me.

"I know you don't see it Elizabeth, but there's more to leading a pack besides being a wolf. You have the ability to command people with your very presence."

I made a noise with my lips. "I could say the same thing about you." My voice came out a whisper, a breath of desire. "And you would more if your dad wasn't such an asshole." I leaned back against the tree and he dropped his hand.

"Don't stop." I put one of his hands on my breast again.

"Oh hell, Elizabeth. Fuck, you're so insatiable sometimes." He grinned. "And fuck if I don't love it."

He bent to his knees and yanked my panties off. I crawled onto his shoulders, using the tree for support as his tongue entered me, stroking my needy clit. I gripped his head, rubbing myself against his face, feeling myself building back up.

His tongue was like magic, stroking and filling and caressing. He knew exactly what I liked. My moans grew louder and he put his hand over my mouth. There was no way he could hold me like this if he wasn't a wolf. I stroked the inside of his hand with my tongue, just like he did to me down *there* and he sucked in his breath.

I exploded again and my orgasm washed over me. Rainbows shot out of my hands and sunshine burst through my toes, making them curl. Or it felt that way anyway.

When I opened my eyes again, his eyes were filled with want and desire. He maneuvered me so that my bare chest was pressing into his and I could feel that he was hard again. I pushed myself on my tiptoes to his ear. "I want you to fuck me again so hard that I see stars."

He clasped me tight and his fingers scraped down my back. "Are you sure?"

I nodded and he leaned over to rummage in his bag, pulling out another condom.

"You brought two condoms?"

He shrugged as he put it on. "You never know."

Then his eyes met mine and I wrapped my legs around him, allowing him to enter me again. He moved slowly at first but I knew that he was holding back. I moved my hips up, pressing the heels of my feet into his back to cling tighter and his hips shot forward.

Damn he was in so deep. A noise came out of me; it was instinctual, almost animalistic and his body exploded against mine, beating me so hard I thought I really would see stars. I moved my hips to his rhythm, leaning back against the tree again to hold my hands over my head, loving his sexual intensity. And then he came and I watched the expression on his face and the warmth of it washed over me.

I did that.

I put that expression on his face.

Me.

He opened his eyes to my satisfied grin. Smiling, he fell over, clasping me to him and I planted my feet back on the ground. His erratic heart thrummed into my body and I ran my hands up and down his naked back, loving the way his skin felt under my fingers. His fingers trailed up the side of my body, tickling the side of my breasts. He slowly turned me around and kissed and tongued the scratches on my back from the tree, his way of apologizing.

Then his bag began to vibrate.

"Oh, hell no. That's not your other girlfriend, is it?"

He grinned. "Maybe. But if it is, I'll just have to tell her I'm occu-pado right now."

I smiled as he leaned over, knowing full well that he didn't have another girlfriend, and his smile slipped off his face.

"Shit. It's my dad."

I frowned and took a step back, allowing him space. I began to get dressed as he answered the phone.

An immediate stream of profanity and anger practically bolted out of the phone. Any attempts to explain himself were cut off until the only sounds he made were affirmative grunts. Then he pressed the end button and put his phone back in his bag. He looked at me with regret. "I gotta run."

I nodded. "No shit, Sherlock."

He laughed, which was what I was going for and he leaned over to kiss me. I wrapped my arms around his neck as he kissed me softly, his hand going to my breast again to stroke it lightly; my shirt was still open since he'd ripped off all my buttons.

He always did that, caressed my breasts without even realizing it. What did that say about him?

"You'd better get going or you're going to have to make me come again. And then I think your dad's going to be really pissed."

He smiled ruefully. "It'd be worth it. To see that look on your face when you come? Definitely."

I grinned and my cheeks flushed. "It wouldn't be worth it for me, your dad's an ass. Who knows what he'd make you do?"

A shadow passed over his face but his smile remained. "As long as I can remember the feel of your skin over mine, it doesn't matter."

I slipped out of his arms and started walking backwards towards my house, still facing him.

"Remember, Elizabeth. No matter what happens tomorrow, you're still destined to be Alpha." He pointed up to the night sky, where the stars shone brilliantly. "The moon determined it."

I waved my hand. "Destiny, smestiny." I blew him a kiss, not wanting to talk about it anymore. His face grew serious for a single second and his eyes bore into mine with an intensity that made me shiver. Then the air around him shimmered and a wolf appeared before me. I eyed him enviously. He made it look so easy.

He picked up his bag with his teeth that held his phone and… condoms apparently, and gave me a final look before he turned and disappeared into the woods.

৯

A HEAVY BODY PRESSED AGAINST ME AND A VOICE TICKLED MY EAR. "Darling daughter, time to get up."

I moaned and moved to my side. "Go way. I don't wanna."

Fingers snaked up to the side of my stomach and I jerked up, grasping at her hands, trying to shove them off me. "Stop! Stop." It was so not fair that I was still ticklish at twenty-four.

My mom was relentless and soon she was climbing over me and I was using my pillows to bat at her head.

Finally she stopped and I pulled her down to lay next to me. I threw my arm around her, snuggling into her neck and tried to go back to sleep. She escaped from under my arm.

"Time to get up. I've brought Carrie over."

My eyes flew open. "You didn't."

She nodded and I groaned. "You just tell her she's not putting blue eyeshadow on me. I'll throw her in the pool if she touches me with that stuff."

She huffed and walked towards my dressers. "She's not that bad."

I closed my eyes again. "She is."

"Well, her family needs the money and they're pack. So."

She didn't need to say anything else. We always took care of pack.

"Elizabeth." My mom stood over me, clutching something in her hand. "I want to give you something."

I sat up intrigued and scooted over so she could sit next to me. She opened her hand and in it she held a blue diamond necklace. The diamond was freaking huge.

My mouth dropped open and I placed my hand on hers, pushing it away. "I can't wear that, mom, I'll just lose it."

21

She smiled. "You won't. I trust you. My mother gave this to me on my birthday many years ago, and now is the time to pass it along to you."

My heart beat wildly in my chest as she twisted the chain around my neck and clasped it at the back. The length of the chain made it rest in the swell of my breasts. "It's too long, I'll get another chain."

She placed her hand over it. "No. This isn't for show. From here on out I want you to wear it. Never take it off, do you hear me?"

I nodded, speechless.

"Keep it tucked inside your shirt or dress, anything you wear. Don't let anyone see it, except after you're married. And then only your mate can see it. And if anyone else happens to see it, just tell them it's something I got you at a flea market. Okay?"

I nodded again; I think this was the first time my mother had rendered me speechless.

"One more thing." Her eyes bore into mine and her seriousness made me swallow hard. "There is only one person, or rather, persons, you can show this to, and I pray that you will never ever have to do it." Her voice caught and I could see fear in her eyes. My eyes widened; I was beginning to be afraid.

"What is it, mom?"

"Hello?" Carrie leaned in through the doorway.

My mom stood up, moving to hide me from Carrie's view. "Carrie." Her voice was warm. "Thank you for coming."

I tucked the necklace under my shirt; it felt heavy. I frowned. What was my mom about to tell me?

Carrie laughed at something my mom said and when I looked up at them, all fear was erased from her features. I opened my mouth to say something but my mom made a motion with her hand.

"Hi, Carrie," I said instead, internally groaning.

"Happy birthday." She held a gift bag towards me. "I brought you a present."

"Um, thanks."

"Open it now, honey." My mom looked eagerly at me, winking.

"Okay." I peeked inside and wished that I'd insisted on waiting. I pulled out a gaudy orange necklace made with plastic rocks.

"I thought this might look good with your birthday dress."

My mouth dropped open in horror. Did she expect me to wear this today? With my gorgeous dress?

My mom took it from me, giving me a warning look. "It's beautiful, Carrie, you're so thoughtful."

"Yeah." I tried to appear enthusiastic. "Thanks so much."

My mom admired it but I could tell that she thought it was horrible as well. "I'm sure Elizabeth would love to wear it."

I wanted to kick her; I even moved my foot back but she stood up and clasped her hands to her chest. "Now, I'm counting on you to make my daughter look her absolute best."

Carrie laughed nervously. "Of course, that's why I'm here."

Carrie walked my mom to the door; she had lots to do to prepare for the gazillion amount of people who were coming. I screamed soundlessly and kicked my bed, vexed at my bad luck. She turned around and I smiled at her.

"Thanks again, Carrie."

She beamed at me. "You're welcome, of course. I wanted to give you something special for your birthday, since you've given me so much." She clapped her hands. "Now, let's get you going. I have a new blue shade that will absolutely bring out the green in your eyes."

I shot up out of the bed. "No!"

Her head jerked back. "What?"

"I mean," I looked around my room, trying to find inspiration to cover my outburst but finding none among the whiteness. "Last time you used the blue. I'd love to try something different this time."

⁊

SCARFACE CLEARLY CAME TO MY BIRTHDAY PARTY WITH AN AGENDA. Everywhere he went he whispered, throwing glances my way with his nose turned up. I was tempted to ask him if he'd recently gotten a nose job, but I didn't want to make things worse so I tried to ignore him.

Instead, I accepted gifts, got cake shoved in my face and even managed to give a speech that made someone laugh so hard that she inhaled champagne through her nose. All around, I considered it a success, except for one thing. Aaron managed to slip away every time we were within three feet of each other.

As the night wore on, the council convened and a burning sensation began to form in my stomach. I held so much tension in my shoulders that they were almost touching my ears. I wasn't allowed inside; none of the potential Alphas were. Only the council members.

What if they decided to replace me?

What if they didn't?

I'd meant what I said to Aaron; I genuinely felt that he would make a better Alpha. Honestly, I didn't know why I couldn't just choose Aaron as my mate and then we could lead the pack together.

Except for the fact that I couldn't choose a mate until I came into my powers.

And that his dad relentlessly pressured Aaron into mating with Olivia, another potential for Alpha and the bane of my existence.

Aaron meant to hold off his dad until I came into my powers. Then I could choose him and his dad couldn't say squat. But as I grew older, coming into my powers seemed to slip through my fingers like a ghost: haunting and dreamlike.

So now I was pacing back and forth in the pantry, biting my nails down to the quick and waiting for their decision. I heard footsteps coming towards me and I stared at the doorway, wide-eyed and my heart pounding in my chest. Had they already made their decision?

Then Aaron appeared and I wanted to rush into his arms but something held me back. Maybe it was because he'd avoided me all night. Maybe it was the look on his face, or the smell of his fear. I'll never know what instinct kept me from going to him but deep down I knew that something was wrong.

"Elizabeth. I was looking for you. Why are you in here?"

"I..." I looked around. "I don't know."

His eyes studied mine. "You look beautiful. I love that dress. And your hair…" He took in a deep breath. "Strawberry shampoo?"

I grinned. "Maybe." Aaron always tried to guess the flavor-of-the-month shampoo.

"Come." He held his hands out. "I brought you something."

I didn't move towards him but it didn't matter, he was already moving deeper into the pantry.

"I thought I might've caught cooties, the way you've been ignoring me."

His hands were on my arms now, his eyes staring into mine. They were dark brown, like melting chocolate. Then he turned me around and began to fiddle with my neck. "My dad reamed me inside and out last night. I couldn't take the chance that he would catch on."

Relief washed over me. "Of course, I'm sorry."

"No, I'm sorry. I should've texted you. My bad."

He turned me back to face him and in his hands was another necklace. Was your twenty-fourth birthday the necklace birthday or something?

He looked at me curiously. "What's this?" I felt a slight tug at my chest as he pulled out the necklace my mother gave me. "Wow, it's gorgeous!"

I grabbed it, panicked, and even though I was really tempted to just tell him, I knew I couldn't. I put it back under my dress, patting it. "It's nothing, just something my mom got me. No big deal."

"Oh." He raised his eyebrow but didn't say anything else.

"It's not real. Just a trinket she found at a rummage sale or something." I pulled the necklace he gave me close to look at it. It was of a silver wolf with a blue gem in its mouth. It was very detailed and beautiful.

"That's me." He pointed to the wolf. "And that's you." He pointed to the gem.

"Why?" Of course he would be the wolf. I felt a small bit of disappointment that even he didn't see me that way.

"I'm the wolf because even when I'm not with you, I'll be with you in wolf spirit. And you're the gem because you are my greatest treasure that I carry with me always."

I looked into his eyes, tears pooling in them. "Thank you. You always know how to make me feel better."

He pulled me to him and wrapped his arms around me, surrounding me with his warmth. "Everything will turn out okay, you'll see."

I nodded, hoping he was right but the twisted feeling in my stomach told me that he was wrong.

Suddenly, noise from the party-goers got really loud and I knew that the meeting was over. It was too soon! Our eyes met for a moment and he squeezed my hand. Then we both walked out of the pantry, trying to appear casual.

Aaron increased his pace to walk ahead of me and just in time because his dad rushed through the kitchen, looking for him. "Aaron." His tone was dark, mean and ugly. Just like him. "Let's go."

His behavior gave me the answer that I so desperately needed and yet I couldn't feel relieved. All I could feel was anger for the wrath that Aaron was sure to endure tonight.

Aaron shot forward, trying to steer his dad away from me and towards the front door, but he didn't move fast enough for his dad.

"I said move it." His hand flew out and landed across Aaron's face with a loud slap. Aaron's head snapped back and he fell backwards.

I rushed forward and caught him, and Aaron clung to me for just a moment and then pushed himself off me.

Scarface's eyes burned into me. "Get away from him you little bitch."

A twisting, burning sensation started in my stomach and spread to my chest. My hands curled into fists; I wanted to punch the lights out of him.

He turned to walk away.

"Garrett." My voice was strong, commanding.

He wanted to ignore me, God he wanted it so bad, but he couldn't. His own body betrayed him as it forced him to look back at me.

"I am your Fated Alpha and you will never speak to me, or touch your son that way again."

His head bowed low under the pressure of my command.

"Do you understand me?"

"Yes, Alpha." His words were practically yanked out of his mouth. He tried to look up but could barely force his head any higher and I could only see the rage that burned in his eyes.

I stepped closer and I could smell the fear coming off him in waves. "If I find out that you've hit him again, I will set up a tribunal to kick you out of the pack and put your son in charge of your house."

That was the worst thing I could do for myself because if Aaron was in charge of his house, he could never be my mate; his responsibilities to his family would be too great. But right now that didn't matter. Alphas always took care of the pack, even if we suffered the consequences. My hand went to the plastic necklace.

Scarface didn't answer but he didn't move either. I looked up at Aaron, feeling a bit of surprise. This was the first time I'd ever used my Alpha powers. But Aaron didn't look at me. I wanted to go to him, to comfort him as he'd comforted me. But I knew I couldn't.

Never show weakness.

"Apologize to your son."

He turned slightly, still keeping his head lower than mine. He spit out the words. "Sorry."

I wasn't going to let him get away with that kind of apology. "Always look someone in the eyes when you apologize."

He tilted his head up to look into Aaron's eyes. "I'm sorry, son."

Aaron nodded his head.

His dad turned back towards me. "Can I go now?"

Suddenly I began to feel very self-conscious, realizing that a crowd had gathered at the kitchen doorway. My dad towered over them all, looking on proudly.

I paused for a moment, wanting to make Scarface sweat but also feeling anxious to take people's eyes off of me. "You can go."

Immediately he stood up and raced towards the door, only glancing slightly back to give me a look mixed with fear and revulsion. Aaron didn't look at me as he left but it didn't bother me. I understood.

Then I turned towards the crowd, wanting to push through them to flee to my bedroom but that would be very un-Alphalike.

"Well." My father clapped his hands together. "I guess you already know the news then." His voice was loud and held a hint that the show was now over and some of the crowd began to thin out back towards the serving table.

A flush crept up my face. "Yeah, I guess I do."

He came over and, weirdly formal, shook my hand. "Congrats, Fated Alpha."

The rest of the council members lined up behind him to shake my hand and congratulate me. Out of the corner of my eye I saw my mother with a strange satisfied look on her face and then she disappeared with a plate of cookies in her hand.

THE EVENING WAS COOL OUTSIDE AND MY DAD AND I STOOD OUT ON the back porch. The party had died down and we were enjoying the fresh night air.

"Jane, come outside with us. Come look at the stars."

"As soon as I finish the dishes and put away the cake."

He sighed. "Forget about the dishes and the cake." He paused. "Or at least leave out a slice; Elizabeth wants another one before she goes to bed." I opened my mouth to protest but he winked and put his finger to his mouth. "Don't say a word."

I ran my finger and my thumb across my lips like a zipper, then pretended to throw away a key.

She called back from the kitchen. "Sure, honey." That's what she always said when she knew it was really for him.

He sat back in his chair and pointed up; I followed his gaze. "Did you know our wolf creatures came from the Goddess Luna."

I sighed. It was going to be *one* of those kinds of nights.

I looked at him, leaning forward in my chair and rested my chin on my hands. "Oh? Do tell." Even though I'd heard the story several times since I was a child.

His lips slid into a grin. "For centuries she watched over the wolves from the night sky as they roamed the earth and she fell in love with Roark, the King of the Wolves. He was strong and smart and brave. But he had never taken a mate. So one day, the Goddess Luna disguised herself as a wolf and approached his pack. As soon as Roark saw her, he instantly fell in love."

I leaned back, taking in the night sky. "And then what happened?"

"Why they married of course, the way mates do and she was his for life. They had several pups together and lived a fulfilling life. But when he grew old, the Goddess grew to be inconsolably sad because she knew that he would die soon."

I listened to the crickets chirp, thinking about growing old with Aaron.

My dad continued, even though I was only halfway listening. "One day, she decided to give the ultimate gift to her love; her necklace that gave her her powers."

I gasped and held my hand to the necklace my mother gave me.

"She revealed her true self to Roark, who was upset at first that she had tricked him for so long. But his love for her was stronger than his anger and so he forgave her. In return, she gave him her necklace and told him that it would give him the desires of his heart."

I was listening closely now. Did this necklace have anything to do with the one my mom just gave me?

"Once he put it on, he transformed into a God, the same form as Luna. And then, they were able to be together for eternity." He looked to the sky. "And that is where we descend from: half-humans, half-wolf, almost as if we were Gods ourselves, with this kind of magical power. And we secretly live among humans, never showing them our true form."

I swallowed hard. "And where is this necklace now?"

He raised his eyebrow. "Well, Roark still wears it, otherwise he'd fall from the sky like a falling star." He imitated an explosion with his hands, grinning.

"Mom gave me a necklace earlier this morning but she never got the chance to tell me what it was for."

He understood my unspoken question and glanced back towards the house. "Jane, are you done yet?"

"Just putting away the cake."

Suddenly my dad leaned forward, sniffing the air with a look of alarm on his face. Then he jumped up, gripping my arm and began to drag me into the house.

"Dad! What's wrong?"

He didn't answer me but pulled me towards his office, calling out. "Jane, get the gun."

There was a crash in the kitchen as my mom dropped the cake and then there was knocking about the kitchen as she raced towards the gun safe.

"Dad, tell me. Tell me!" I was trying to hurry but he was pulling me so fast, super fast, that I couldn't keep up.

"Elizabeth, get in the safe room." We were in his office now and he pushed the code into the keypad on the hidden panel. Metal scraped against metal as the door unlocked, taking only a couple minutes but they were the longest minutes of my life.

I gripped his shoulders, fear making my hands shake. "You and mom have to come inside with me. I won't go in there without you."

Then I heard it, the noise that my dad heard long before me. The sound of several cars pulling up our driveway. My eyes widened in fear. "It's Scarface, isn't it? He's come to kill you."

"I don't know." He was afraid, too. I could see it in his eyes and even smell it. "But I know he didn't come to have a discussion. Not with that many cars."

The front door slammed open and footsteps bounded down the hallway; I counted at least twenty pair of feet.

"Robert," Scarface's voice boomed through the hallway from the direction of the front door. "I challenge you as Alpha of the South-eastern White Tooth pack."

The safe room door finally opened and my dad shoved me inside. I clung to his arm. "No, Dad, you have to come with me! Mom!" I screamed as loud as I could.

A loud boom shook the walls and I couldn't help but grin. Mom had access to the rifle. Dad took advantage of my distraction to shove me inside the room and slam the door shut. It only took a second to lock and I pounded on the door but it wouldn't open.

Once the safe room door closed, it wouldn't open again for four hours. I heard dad punch in the keypad again and the panel hiding the door closed. Then he looked into the hidden camera by the door and kissed it. "I love you."

Crying out, I screamed for him to let me out, for him to come inside, to get mom but he disappeared from sight. I scrambled to the monitors and flipped on the screens frantically; there were cameras all over the house. It took a moment for everything to boot up but I could finally see my dad.

He was on the phone.

On the phone! Who was he calling and why wasn't he protecting my mom?

I searched the screens, looking for her. There were wolves everywhere, much more than I originally thought. They roamed the house tearing apart pillows, jumping on the countertops to shove everything off and peeing on the walls.

I couldn't see my mom, where was she?

And then I saw her foot. Just her foot and my heart leaped out of my chest. It was laying on the floor and she wasn't moving. The wood flooring underneath her was wet.

"Mom! Mom! Get up!" I knew she couldn't hear me, the room was soundproofed, but I couldn't stop myself.

I looked back to the office to look at my dad, he was still on the phone but he was yelling at it. Then Scarface came into the room and I screamed at my dad to turn around. But of course, he couldn't hear me.

Scarface grinned; it was the grin of the predator who knew his prey was dead. I scrambled to the door and jerked at the handle but I knew it would do no good. I ran back to the screen. Scarface and my dad were fighting it out.

They'd already shifted and I couldn't see what was happening, they were moving too fast. Blood and fur was spraying through the air. Finally my dad landed on top of him, his teeth clenching Scarface's throat.

And then, he hesitated.

It would've only taken a second to crush his neck but he hesitated; he didn't want to kill him.

Another wolf, one so black it was almost blue, jumped on my dad. I stared into the screen; I'd never seen this wolf before.

I watched in horror as he knocked my dad over. Tears poured down my face.

It wasn't fair. They were supposed to fight one-on-one.

They both ganged up on him, clawing and biting at my dad until he was on his back. The black wolf went in for the kill, trying to tear out his neck but my dad growled at him, snapping his teeth, and the black wolf backed up, afraid.

My dad tried to turn to his feet but the black wolf stepped on his neck while Scarface, the motherfucker, ripped out my dad's belly and began to eat the insides. Then, the other wolf grabbed his neck and broke it.

I cried out and turned my face, I couldn't watch them. My whole body felt numb and I fell to the floor, curling up in a ball.

They killed my parents. They waited until everyone was gone and then they came back.

They were cowards!

I wanted to rip them to shreds.

I crawled to the monitor and covered the spot where my dad lay so I wouldn't have to look at it. The wolves were gone from the office; the handle to the phone lay on the floor. I scanned the other screens. They were racing through the rooms and I knew they were looking for me.

I wanted to run out of the room, call out for them to kill me.

They'd already killed my parents.

I recognized some of the wolves from my own pack.
They'd betrayed my father; they'd betrayed me.
I had nothing left to live for.
But the door wouldn't let me out.
I fell to the floor again, my sobs wrenching my body.
I had nothing left.

3

*B*eep.

My eyes opened. I must have cried myself to sleep. Or passed out.

The door. That's what the beep was. The door could open.

I went back to the screens. My dad was missing and I could no longer see my mom's foot. As far as I could tell, the house was empty except for one lone wolf, shifted back to his human form. He was sitting on the couch, eating leftover cake and watching tv.

I stared at him, open mouthed. How could he?

He'd just participated in the slaughter of my parents and now he was eating my fucking cake? The cake my *mom* made me? I would kill him.

I pushed the button to open the door and waited for the locks to disengage. A numbness moved over my body and I felt my mind sharpen. I could smell the coppery smell of blood; it was so strong it almost made me gag.

When the door opened, I slid it open silently, then the hidden panel.

I could smell the wolf from here.

Something must've happened. Even though my senses were stronger than the average human, I'd never been so alert in my life.

Just as I started towards the hallway, I spotted the blood stain on the floor.

I stared at it in fear; that's where they killed my dad.

I went to it and pressed my hand on it, silent tears streamed down my face.

I love you, Dad!

I only waited for a moment, and then I turned back towards the hallway, ready for revenge.

❧

THEY'D LEFT AN UNFAMILIAR MAN TO WATCH FOR MY RETURN. HE wasn't much of a watch guard; he'd turned the tv on too loudly and he was yelling at the game. The stupid oaf couldn't hear me as I slipped from the room.

I moved silently to the gun safe; the door hung open. The safe for our valuables was open too, empty.

The rifle was gone but the Glock .45 was still in it. I slid it out, trying to be quiet even though he probably wouldn't hear me. I checked the chamber, it was empty. I slid out the magazine of bullets - it was full. I grabbed another box of bullets, just in case I needed it. Then I took the safety off and loaded the chamber.

THE WATCH GUARD DIDN'T EVEN SEE ME COMING BUT HE FELT IT AS soon as I was there. I pressed the gun to the back of his head.

"Don't move." He froze and I smelled a bit of piss. "You killed my family. Prepare to die."

I don't know why I quoted 'The Princess Bride' but it seemed fitting.

He tried to turn but I pulled the trigger and the bullet went right through his head, spraying blood and brain matter over my mother's

35

couch. I didn't even have time to think about what I'd just done; I heard feet running towards the front door.

There must be more men outside.

I had to make a split-second decision; stay and shoot them until I ran out of bullets - I probably wouldn't have time to reload. I didn't know how many there were or what kind of weapons they had.

I decided to run.

𓅓

THE BACKYARD WAS EMPTY AND I RACED TOWARDS THE TREES, BITING MY tongue as the sticks and rocks scratched at my feet. I was well into the woods when I heard them in my backyard.

I zigzagged through the trees, still clutching the gun and bullets, and said a prayer of thanks that I knew this forest like the back of my hand.

Damn, I wished I could shift like I'd never wished before. Branches flew at me, catching in my hair and tearing my dress. I pushed them away, not bothering to be quiet because it wouldn't matter anyway. Wolves could hear the slightest snap.

Every noise around me was heightened; I could hear the birds that took flight and the chipmunks that scrambled to their holes as I crashed through the woods. I could also hear three wolves on my tail so close that it felt like their breath blew on my ear.

I stayed on the path, knowing that if I went off it, they would have a major advantage over me, although I didn't have an endgame. Where was I going? And what would I do when I got there?

The only thing I could think of was the creek, maybe they would lose my scent if I followed it down. If I could outrun them that long.

My arms pumped, my legs flew through the air and my lungs were about to explode, I was running so hard. Then I heard the sound of the water flowing and I knew that I was going to make it.

The wolves behind me had fallen back, completely baffling me but I had no time to think about it. I came around the bend in the trail and could see the creek beyond. I pushed harder, willing my feet to go faster and then a dark grey wolf leaped from the forest onto the trail. I didn't recognize him.

I skidded to a stop and turned back. Two other wolves led up the trail that way. They must be from the new pack.

I lifted my gun and stepped back so I could see them.

"Leave me alone or I'll shoot." My hand shook as the realization that I'd already killed a man with this gun came over me.

I'd only used one bullet.

I had sixteen left.

The wolves didn't stop and they didn't shift back into human form. They meant to kill me.

I steadied my hand, looked through my sight and shot three shots rapid fire towards the largest wolf. Thirteen left.

They began to sprint towards me, moving so fast that I only hit one in the shoulder.

I unloaded my gun on them, swiping the gun for maximum effect and two of them went down. I turned towards the other one, arm held out, and jumped in fear as he leaped towards me. I shot my last bullet and it hit him in the chest. He fell to the ground.

The smell of blood was overwhelming and I bent over and threw up cake and strip steak. Breathing heavily, I wiped my mouth and went to check on the wolves. All three were dead.

❧

I SAT ON THE COLD GROUND, DRIPPING WET FROM THE CREEK AND MY own tears. My dad. Dead. My mom. Dead. I'd killed four people.

The gun lay next to me; I'd already reloaded it and was waiting for them. Night had already passed and the sun was beginning to rise. Even though I was hiding in a cove of rocks, I knew that they would find me; it was only a matter of time. I'd shoot as many as I could and then I would die.

There were footsteps outside and I shot to my feet, my gun held out in front of me. Aaron stepped forward and for a second, my heart stopped.

I cocked the gun and he froze. "Lizzy."

"How many did you bring?"

Aaron's face broke, his anguish clear. He had a black eye and he favored his left foot. "I didn't."

"How many, Aaron? How many people came with you? Did you tell them you could get me to come out? Is your dad here?"

His voice was desperate. "I had nothing to do with this, I swear. I swear it."

"Did you know he was going to do it?"

"I didn't know."

I still held my gun out. "Liar! You've been acting different lately. Distant. I could even feel your fear yesterday. Is that why you wouldn't talk to me at the party? Cuz you didn't want to be seen associating with the daughter of a fallen Alpha?"

"Listen, Lizzie," he tried to take a step further but I held my gun steady, giving him a look that showed him I meant it and he stopped. "You have to believe me. I had no idea."

"Where were you then, Aaron?" My voice broke and sobs threatened to overtake me. "You were the one person I trusted the most. Where were you? You could've helped him. You could've saved my mom."

"Lizzy, you have to listen to me, they'll find you soon. They're already searching the woods near here. He's taken over the pack. Even those that don't want to follow him are too afraid to stand up to him."

I shook the gun at him, screaming. "Where were you, Aaron?"

Aaron fell to his knees and his sobs ripped from his mouth. He climbed on his hands towards me, his face dragging on the ground, and I knew that he did it to show his absolute obeisance to me. He saw me as the Alpha now.

"I couldn't come, I swear it, Lizzy." He was at my feet now, his face pressing against them. "I wanted to. He's telling everyone he beat your dad in the challenge for Alpha, but I know your dad and my dad. Your dad was stronger and faster than my dad. I just know my dad didn't fight fairly. "

"He didn't. There was another wolf, a black one. And he brought at least twenty more with him."

His mouth dropped open then he shook his head. "If I would've known what they were going to do, I would've…"

"What, Aaron? Why couldn't you come? What would you have done?" My voice was cold.

He looked up at me, a pitiful state. "I would've killed my dad." His eyes were glacial, and I knew that he spoke the truth. "He knew. Somehow he knew about us. He must have suspected and then when you defended me, he knew the truth. I couldn't come because he locked me in a cage."

At this, I lost anything holding me together and dropped the gun and fell to the ground. He pulled me into his arms, clinging to me like a lifeline. "He let me out this morning. I know he's tracking me to get to you, that's why you have to go."

"How long has this been going on?"

Aaron looked away. "It doesn't matter now. What matters is that you need to get away. He'll be here soon."

"How many times has he locked you in a cage? How long has he been doing this to you? Tell me the truth, Aaron."

He looked into my eyes and I could see his pain, and it tore into my heart. "Two years."

"Aaron, why didn't you tell me?"

"I couldn't tell you."

"Why not?"

"Because I was embarrassed. And because he's my dad."

"You could've told me. I told you everything, why didn't you trust me? I would've done something." I felt like the most selfish person in the world. This whole time I thought that he was distancing himself from me because I couldn't shift, or because his dad was pressuring him to marry Olivia. I'd never once thought it was because *his* life was screwed up.

"You lied to me about the necklace."

I put my hand to my chest. I'd forgotten about my mom's necklace.

I was still wearing that stupid plastic one. I felt lower and relief flowed through me, my mom's necklace was still there. But Aaron's wasn't.

"Your necklace, it's go—"

He held it up and I grabbed it. "You found it."

He nodded. "It was hanging from a tree branch."

I frowned and put it back around my neck; somehow the clasp hadn't broken. "How did you find me anyway?"

"You don't know?"

I shook my head. "No, I... Did you track me from the creek?"

He shook his head. "No. They lost your trail from there. But look around, Lizzie. Do you even recognize where you are?"

I looked around and realized that we were in the exact same spot I'd screwed Aaron last time we went hiking. That seemed like a lifetime ago.

I put my hand to my mom's necklace again; it felt warm. "How did you know I lied about the necklace?"

He rolled his eyes. "Cuz you can't lie for shit to me, I know you too well. That and," he swallowed hard, "cuz my dad's looking for it."

My eyes widened. "He is? Why?"

He shrugged. "I don't know, but you can never let him have it. I don't know why, but he wants it real bad." He looked into my eyes. "Enough to kill for it." I nodded, feeling my tears fall down my face. He'd killed my parents for it. I gripped my hand around it and squeezed it tight.

Suddenly he sat up and put his hands on the side of my face to stare into my eyes. "You have to go, Lizzy, they're going to be here soon."

I shook my head. "I have no where to go. They'll find me at my house."

"I brought one of my cars, the black Mustang. It's fast and I disabled the GPS so he can't track you. I grabbed as much cash as I could find, it's under the driver's seat."

"But where am I going to go?"

He stood up and, giving me the gun, he pulled me with him, and we headed towards the forest. "Anywhere. Mexico, Sweden. Anywhere you want."

I gripped his hand. "I'll go if you come with me. I can't do this by myself. I love you, I want you with me."

We were silent for a second; I'd never told him I loved him and we were both momentarily stunned.

"I can't. I have to stay for my mom and my sisters."

I shook my head. "We'll come back for them later. Come with me now, Aaron, please." I hated begging him but I would do it.

He gripped my shoulders, shaking them. "I can't Elizabeth, can't you see? I don't know what he'll do to my mom if I leave."

He let me go and I was crying again. Dammit, I was so tired of crying. He began to pull me out of the cove of rocks and towards the edge of the forest.

"Fine, I'll stay then. I'm the Alpha now, the council voted on it."

He shook his head. "There is no council. He disbanded it."

"But…" I was at a loss. How could my life have changed so drastically in just a few hours? Why didn't my dad listen to me? I knew that fat-faced fucker would kill us, why didn't he listen? "I'll challenge him. I'll fight."

"No, Elizabeth."

I stopped, forcing him to halt. I locked eyes with him. "I'll kill him. He killed my parents, and I have nothing left, Aaron."

He blinked and I knew that I'd hurt his feelings. I didn't care. Then he shook his head. "No."

"Why not? Give me a good reason."

His voice came out desperate. "Because you can't fight him if you can't shift, Elizabeth."

There. That was it.

The elephant in the forest.

And he was right.

"Fuck, fuck, fuck!!" I stamped my feet. "I hate that motherfucker."

He took my hand, leading me again and we moved down the path towards the road; we were almost there. "Aaron, you have to fight him. You can't let him do that to you anymore, to your family. He has to be stopped."

"I know." His voice was quiet but I knew that he was serious. I knew that he would kill his dad if he could. Suddenly we heard the sound of running wolf paws and Aaron began to run, pulling me with him.

We ran off the path, taking the shortest route to the car as we heard a tree branch snap to the left. Finally reaching the car, he opened the door and placed the gun inside the door. Then he took my face in his hands again and pulled me to him. His kiss was desperate, needy, and filled with longing and despair. Then he pushed me down onto the black leather seat and the new car smell filled my nose.

"I've loved you for five years, Lizzy. I will find you again."

Then he slammed the door and I started it up; it roared loudly. Out of the corner of my eye I saw several wolves running towards us. I hesitated to go but he slammed his hand on the top of the car, yelling at me to leave. I slammed my foot on the gas. The car jerked forward and stalled out, throwing me off. I started the car again and this time gently pressed the gas, switching gears properly and the car moved forward.

I looked in my rearview mirror. He was standing in the middle of the road, his clothes shredding to his feet and he was shifting. Then he was standing on all fours facing them. The pack ran into the street knocking him over and I saw a golden red-haired wolf pounce on him.

I cried out, but kept going, knowing that Aaron would kill me himself if I stopped. I slammed my foot on the gas and the car shot forward as the tires peeled off the pavement.

I pushed the gas pedal to the floor. Appearing out of nowhere, the largest freaking bird thingee I've ever seen slammed into hood, leaving a large dent and surprising the crap out of me.

4

I screamed and came to a stop. That was not a bird.
That was a…

I couldn't even think it.

It looked like a damn dragon. I said it out loud to myself just to let myself know how freaking insane I'd become. Iridescent blue scales covered the whole length of his muscular body, leading up to sharp eyes that studied me through my windshield.

My heart thumped in my chest. His head was as big as the length of my body, and a shiver went up my spine. This thing could eat me in one bite.

And yet, I had the eerie sensation that it was almost human. Or, had human thoughts anyway. As if it was having human thoughts about… me.

I felt a sudden sensation that even though my life was spiraling out of control, it was going in the exact place that it needed to be. That I wasn't meant for the world that was given to me but for one that was greater. Larger. One that included the dragon before me.

Oh, hell.

I'm not some motherfucking hot blonde girl from a tv show.

Suddenly, I remembered the pack of wolves behind me and I revved the car, trying to warn it to fly it away. Finally, it broke its stare on me and stood up on its hind legs, reaching its long neck of shimmering blue scales to gaze at the chaos behind me. Its feet had sharp claws twice as long as my middle finger and they cut through the metal of the car as it climbed to the top. The sound of it scraped at the inside of my skull.

I looked in my review mirror and my heart leapt in my throat. The pack was so close. Now they were approaching warily, their focus on the dragon. I took off again, not caring about the dragon; it would just have to take a hint. I had to get out of there.

As soon as I moved forward, the dragon spread out its humongous wings - the wings reaching a lot further than the span of my car - and flew behind me.

I shifted gears and sped down the road, forcing my mind to focus on the road ahead. A glance in my mirror saw that the dragon had landed in the middle of the road and was fighting off the wolves. My mouth dropped open and my foot came off the gas. I turned in my seat.

It breathed out small shots of flame and flapped its wings towards the pack. Most of the wolves were backing up, hairs on their back hackled up and teeth snapping.

Some of the braver ones shot forward and were met with the threat of becoming barbecue roadkill. Two of them managed to make it through and were tearing at the dragon's wings.

The dragon shot up in the air, bringing the wolves with it. The length of it, from head to tail, was as tall as the surrounding pines. It flew high into the air and flung the wolves to the ground. One of them landed in a roll, spinning off of the street and towards the woods. The other one landed on its back and was still.

I pulled the emergency brake and got out of my car, staring in shock at the sight. As if I needed one more thing to add to this unbelievable day.

"Elizabeth."

I turned, startled, to see a black SUV Escalade backing up next to me. A blond haired, green-eyed man, with kissable lips, opened his door and stood just outside of the passenger door.

I'd been so enthralled with the dragon that I hadn't even noticed his car approach. I grabbed my gun and held it towards him. "Don't come a step any closer." I cocked it. I was not playing.

I glanced towards the driver's seat of his SUV - there was someone else driving, obviously, but I couldn't see him very well because the lighting was too dim.

"Elizabeth, your dad called us. He asked us to come save you."

I narrowed my eyes at him. "I don't believe you."

He held his hands up and took a step towards me. I held both hands to the gun, steadying it.

He stopped. "Your dad is Robert, Alpha of the Southeastern White Tooth pack. He's known my trainer, Edward, since they met at Washington Lee University in Virginia. Your mom is Jane. They got married in the Spring, about twenty-five years ago, and Edward gave him a silver onyx ring for a wedding present. You're an only child and you live in the house beyond this forest."

I felt a cold douse of shock. How did he know all this?

"Robert and Edward stayed in touch throughout the years and last night your dad called Edward. Your dad said that you need help, that he thought he was going to die and that you needed to be protected. We came here to help you." He held out his hand and his green-as-meadow eyes stared into mine. "Please. We can help you."

The road under my feet was beginning to burn from the dragon fighting my pack still raging behind me. I wanted to get in his car, to leave this world behind and drive away to a world where none of this existed. Where my parents were still alive. But with him?

He ran his hands through his hair in a frustrated gesture. "You're in succession as future Alpha but you can't shift."

Always with that, always with the Alpha-daughter-can't-shift-crap. Didn't I have any other redeeming qualities that people could talk about instead? Like maybe my kissable lips? Aaron thought they were anyway.

At that thought, I glanced towards the pack, wondering what had happened to him. I could barely see him beyond the dragon's wings; he was muzzled like a dog and guarded by several wolves. At least he was still alive.

"Elizabeth, we need to go now. I don't know how long Hunter will be able to hold them off." His eyes bore into mine. "Without killing them, that is. They're still your pack after all."

Ugh.

"Fine. But I'm bringing my gun."

He shrugged his shoulders and then stepped beyond his door to open mine. I reached back into the Mustang and grabbed the leather bag that held Aaron's cash under the seat: I wouldn't be without a way to escape. I scanned the car once more and couldn't find a single thing that reminded me of home to bring with me. I pushed down the sadness that clung to me; I would have to be brave now.

My parents gave their lives for mine.

I would do them right.

I would be brave.

I turned and jumped into the SUV, sullying the tan leather seats with dirt and pine needles, and with a final glance, said goodbye to the woods I once called home.

❦

As soon as I shut the door, the SUV shot off and soon we were flying down the road, leaving everyone behind. Kissable lips held his phone to his ear, waiting for someone to pick up.

"Tell me." I could clearly hear the deep voice that answered the phone.

"We have her."

The person who answered the phone sighed in relief. "Adhere to protocol. Make sure no one follows you."

"Of course." Kissable Lips sounded annoyed. Then the line was silent and Lips threw his phone on the dashboard. He turned towards me and I gripped the gun in my lap tighter.

"I'm Christian." He held his hand towards me and smiled warmly; I

46

eyed his hand with mistrust. He pulled it back and ran his hand through his hair. "This is Avery."

Avery, the mysterious driver, nodded towards me, his eyes meeting mine in his rearview mirror. Bare chested, I could see several tattoos snake around his defined, olive-skinned arms. He didn't have any shoes on. He didn't say anything to me, but his serious burnt sienna-colored eyes studied mine in the mirror.

I looked away first and stared out the window, ignoring any of Christian's attempts at conversation. I suddenly remembered the fairy tales my dad used to tell me about dragons as a child. He said they used to roam the lands until the knights killed many of them off. Then one day, the King of the dragons saved a magic Fairy and in return, the Fairy put a spell on the King which allowed him to change his shape to a human form. This allowed them to blend in with the humans, where they were able to hide in plain sight. Turns out there was a catch, as there usually is when dealing with the fae. The catch was that the gene for the change was rare and not every child born had it. That, combined with the fact that impregnating a woman with a dragon was hard as hell to do. Eventually they died off.

Or had they?

Could the stories my dad told me actually be true?

The spit stuck in my throat and I tried to swallow it down but it was just stuck, my throat impossibly dry.

I could never ask him now, could I?

My tears threatened to spill but I pushed them away quickly. I would not show weakness.

Scarface had fulfilled my prophecy, living up to his nickname and now I was the little wolf running off to the jungle with Timone and Pumbaa.

A slow burn boiled in my stomach and spread to my chest. I knew the truth, that Garrett had taken over the pack illegally and because of that, I was a threat. He wouldn't stop looking for me until he'd killed me.

The only way I would get out of this alive was to challenge him for Alpha of the pack.

But how could I challenge him if I couldn't shift?

The necklace at my neck glowed with a soft warmth, and I put my hand to it, remembering my mother's words. Never show it to anyone. Except for… someone else. But who? Who was that?

It didn't matter anymore. I was alone, and knew that I would have to come into my powers, or I would die.

It was as simple as that.

§.

WE DROVE FOR A LONG TIME AND THE MORNING SHIFTED INTO LATE afternoon. We didn't stop to eat, only to pump gas once and then we were off again. The further we drove from my family home in Tennessee, the more concerned I became about the new men in my life. They spoke little but sat in a comfortable silence, only speaking to discuss directions. I caught Avery studying me occasionally in the rearview mirror but he glanced away quickly. Christian even fell asleep and I watched him warily.

Anyone could get information about my parents, right? The only thing that kept me from completely freaking out was the mention of my dad's ring. You would have to be in close contact with my dad to even know about the ring.

But 'contact' didn't necessarily mean that they were friends.

As we drove, my thoughts grew deeper and deeper. My mom's necklace grew even hotter but I was afraid to take it off. Sweat began to drip down the side of my face, under my arms and in between my breasts. I was so hot that I was tempted to pull off my dress, now torn and muddy from my chase through the woods, and throw it out the window.

It would never recover anyway.

Not that I wanted to keep it; it would only serve as a memory of the worst night of my life.

I felt the elevation of the land rise and had to move my jaw to make my ears pop. I looked behind me; there was no one. I peeked out the window, looking towards the sky and could see the dragon following us through the trees.

We turned off and drove down a gravel road which ended at a large and beautiful cabin-home. There was a motorcycle parked at the end of the driveway but there was no other sign of any living thing. Fear gripped my gut; we would be alone. In a secluded cabin in some remote part of the mountains. It sounded like the plot of a bad movie to me.

As we got closer to the house, I gripped my gun and leather bag tightly, ready to bolt. As soon as the car stopped, I jumped out and sprinted towards the woods.

"Elizabeth! Stop!" Christian's words barely registered as I raced through the woods, jumping over fallen logs and the last word I heard him say was directed at the sky. "Hunter!"

I kept on running, startling a deer with her two fawns. They ran down the hill, their white tails flashing. I pushed myself as hard as possible but I was tiring quickly. It was an effort to raise each foot. How long had it been since I'd eaten?

I heard a noise behind me; it was too heavy to be a deer and it was coming closer to me. I pressed harder, throwing my bag onto the ground because it was just holding me back. I realized too late that I had no idea where I was going. Every tree here seemed like the rest.

Suddenly large arms surrounded my waist and I fell to the ground, dropping my gun.

"No!"

We rolled on the ground and I tried to twist out of his arms but he held me tight. We finally stopped and he shifted himself so that he was on top of me, holding me with his thighs.

"Stop, Elizabeth. We're just trying to help."

My heart thudded in my chest as I stared into his clear blue eyes. They were like a crystal clear ocean on a cloudless day. *Traitor*, I told my hormones. I squirmed, trying to slip out of his hold but he was too strong. His thighs were like thick oak trees and they surrounded my whole body.

Suddenly, I felt so weak, like I couldn't even hold my head up anymore. I lay my head back relaxing; it was pointless to fight against him anyway. I closed my eyes; I hadn't slept all night. I would just rest for a second.

&.

A COOLNESS SURROUNDED ME AND MY EYES WERE SO HEAVY I COULDN'T open them. I was on a soft mattress and a down blanket covered me.

"She's been asleep for almost twenty hours, shouldn't we wake her up?" It was a rough voice.

"Let her sleep. She'll need her energy." The same voice from the woods. It was commanding, in charge. I recognized a leader when I heard one.

Rough Voice sighed. "Alright, you're in charge." There was a pause, then Rough Voice continued. "How long are we going to be here?"

"It depends on the information that Easton gives us. He's keeping an eye on the trackers we put on her pack. He'll let us know if they get too close."

"If we're here for long, we'll need to update the house. Replace the broken cameras and sensors in the woods."

"We'll wait a couple of days. If it looks like we'll be here for long, we'll do that."

I considered turning on my side but didn't want to alert them that I was awake. I realized I was shivering; it was so cold. I gripped my blanket tighter and pulled it up to my neck. Then the memory of what happened rushed over me and a sob tore from my throat.

I would never see my parents again. I couldn't even have a funeral for them.

If I didn't learn to shift, I was going to die.

It felt like there was a hole in my chest where someone had ripped my heart out.

I couldn't contain my sobs now, I folded myself in a fetal position and cried, wishing I could fold myself so small that I would just disappear.

The bed moved and there was a gentle hand on my arm. "Shhh, it's going to be okay." Rough voice. The bed shook again; he'd jumped up.

"Holy crap, she's hot as hell."

Footsteps came towards me and a cool hand pressed against my forehead for a quick moment. "She was warm earlier but not this hot. We have to cool her down and fast. Get some ice and I'll put her in the tub."

The blanket came off me and rough but gentle hands moved over my body, pushing me onto my stomach. I felt a tug at my back and then my back was cool. He was trying to unzip my dress.

ॐ

MY EYES SHOT OPEN AND I FLIPPED ONTO MY BACK TO FACE THE MAN who trapped me in the woods. Hunter.

"Don't." I rubbed my hands up my arms and then tried to pull the blanket back on. "It's so-oo cold." My teeth were chattering.

"That's because you have a high fever. At least a hundred and seven. We have to get you cooled down right now."

I shook my head but he ignored me, grabbing my hands to pull me to my feet. "Come on. You don't have a choice in the matter."

As soon as I stood up, the floor rushed towards me and he wrapped his arms around me, holding me up. I tried to pick up my foot but it wouldn't mind my brain.

Sighing, he leaned over and pulled me into his arms, picking me up like a baby. Passing several rooms, he took me to a bathroom and sat me on the toilet. While he started running the water in the pedestal tub, I looked around the room, still shaking. I could barely form complete thoughts but my instincts burned through my mind enough to warn me of pending danger; I still wasn't sure if I could trust them. I looked for anything I could use as a weapon.

The back wall was a row of windows and the tub had a clear view of the private forest behind the house. The rest of the walls were a happy light-blue, and the ceiling tiles ran along the whole bathroom.

There was nothing on the counter, except for a toothbrush still in its packaging. I could use that if there was nothing else.

Then I noticed a freestanding toilet paper caddy next to the toilet. It had a pointed end, maybe I could use it as a weapon? But what would I do with the toilet paper?

I shook my head; I wasn't making any sense.

Suddenly, I remembered my mom's necklace. I slipped it off and hid it inside one of the toilet paper rolls.

The floors were a dark brown marble and my eyes swept up the floor to look at Hunter's back. His blond hair fell down over his eyes and his cheekbones looked like they were cut from the finest marble available. He could easily make the front cover of every teen heart-throb magazine. He didn't have a shirt on either and his muscles rippled as he moved over the tub, testing the temperature of the water.

Satisfied, he left it running and came back towards me. His look was appraising and I felt his stare burn a hole right through me. He walked with the confidence of a man who knew exactly how to kill a person in three-seconds. Power pulsed through his body, oozing through every pore and it sent a shiver up my body. I felt a mixture of awe at the sexy man in front of me and a feeling that I didn't exactly trust him.

I formed my hand into a fist, I might not have a weapon on me but at least I could pack a punch. My eyes were still heavy but I tried to keep them open.

"Come on, time to get in the tub." He held his hand out to me.

I gripped my hands to my chest; afraid he would try to take my dress off. "I can do it."

He stopped and waited for me to stand up.

"By myself."

Shrugging he moved towards the back wall and leaned against it, crossing his hands over his chest. "Whatever you say, Princess."

It took two seconds before my face was about to meet the floor again and his arms were around me, stopping me. He growled. "I'm going to take this dress off, then get you in that tub. Don't fight me on this."

Dammit, his commanding voice was so sexy. I nodded, giving in, trying to keep my teeth from chattering. "Kay."

He turned me around, steadying me on my feet and his hands burned through my skin as they moved softly from my arms to my back. He unzipped my dress deliberately and the cool air hit my back, sending a shiver down my spine. Then he undid the hook at my bra and slipped it off my shoulders. I closed my eyes as his hands went to my undies and my breath caught in my throat as he pulled them down slowly. As soon as I stepped out of them, he guided me to the tub and helped me inside, then shut off the faucet.

The water was a shock to my body and I gasped. "If I'd have known your water heater didn't work, I'd have made Christian stop by the hardware store to grab one on our way here."

He frowned. "You need to cool down."

"Lukewarm water would cool me down enough." I'd read that somewhere on the internet and the internet never lies.

He shook his head. "You need it cold to get your temperature down."

"But it's too cold."

"It just feels that way."

I tried to protest but he cut me off with a growl.

"Shut up, Elizabeth. It doesn't matter how cold the water is; I'll do whatever it takes to get your fever down."

As if on cue, Avery walked into the bathroom with a large bucket of ice. This must be Rough Voice.

"Sorry it took so long." He wasn't talking to me.

Hunter shook the ice into the water and I shivered violently. Frowning, Hunter ran his hands up my arms and Avery sat near my legs, rubbing them. Then Avery's eyebrows furrowed as he studied the scratches on the soles of my feet. I pulled them back into the water, not wanting him to fuss.

"You'll cool down in a moment and then we'll put some clothes on you. You'll feel better soon, I promise." Hunter looked at Avery. "Did you get her clothes?"

He nodded. "They're still in the motorcycle."

"Go grab them and then tell Christian to make some food."

Avery left and the ice started having an effect on the water. I pulled my legs towards my chest, trying to keep myself warm, but I was still shaking.

Hunter touched my arm. "Dammit, now you're too cold."

"I tol—ld you." I wasn't bragging or anything.

He brushed his hair out of his eyes. "I've never done this on my own before."

"Done what?"

Hunter stood up and unzipped his jeans. When he revealed his boxers, I looked away quickly.

"You're not getting in here with me." I pulled my arms around my knees tighter.

"Hush." He grabbed my shoulders and pushed me forward. I could feel his smooth skin slide under mine as he got behind me in the tub.

"Just relax, Elizabeth." With his presence in the tub, I immediately felt better. He wrapped his arms around me and pulled me to his chest. I couldn't help but notice how firm his muscles were and warmth shot through my body. He hummed something softly that I didn't recognize and I found myself relaxing in his embrace.

"Tell me something."

"Mmm?" He put his chin on my shoulder and his breath ran down the front of my chest, making my nipples perk.

"How did you know where to find me? By the road."

"We didn't. We'd been looking all night but we had to keep our distance so your pack wouldn't see us. But we kept our eye on them and they finally led us to you." His thumbs made small circles on my stomach and I flushed, very aware of the way they stroked my skin.

"Why do you care so much? I mean, you don't even know me."

He paused for a long moment and I thought that I'd said something wrong. I turned my face towards him and he was staring stonily at the wall. Then he glanced at me and his eyes softened.

"You've never seen me before?"

I shook my head, wondering what he could mean. Did I ever see him in college? Or maybe at work?

"Did I—"

He pulled me back into his embrace. "No, it's okay. I was just thinking that you looked familiar. But even if I've never met you, you're still pack."

I furrowed my eyebrows. "But I'm not part of your pack."

And then I felt his right shoulder go up in a shrug and the water dripped from his arm as he traced my arm. "Sometimes pack isn't just about what we shift into or how we're born. Sometimes packs are forged through bonds, whether blood or not."

It was quiet except for the drip of the water as I processed this. "Tell me something else."

"Yes?" He touched the side of my face, brushing my hair out of the way and my heartbeat quickened. I was definitely heating up; did he notice the way my cheeks reddened at his touch?

"Are you really real?"

His laugh was deep and came from deep within his chest. I liked it.

"I mean, are you really a dragon shifter? I didn't know they existed."

"We rarely expose ourselves; there aren't many of us left so we have to remain in secrecy for the most part."

I was quiet for a while and my eyes began to droop as a dreamy sensation came over me. Finally I answered him. "I know that."

He expelled a breath. "And how did you know that?"

"My dad told me." I leaned my head back and he shifted his body so that I was pressed against his chest again. I closed my eyes as his fingers caressed my stomach again; he made me feel so... sexy. My wolf wanted to stretch out and be stroked like a freaking cat. I imagined his tongue running over my body and I shivered.

He rubbed my arms again, thinking that I was growing cold. "You're not making any sense."

I shrugged. "I know."

"Dragon shifters mostly live in Aerwyna, a place in Europe but we live all over the world."

"I've never heard of that."

"That's because it's a magical place, like a Cinderella story."

I humphed. "I hate that stupid story."

He chuckled. "Why am I not surprised?" Suddenly he leaned forward again and my eyes shot open.

"Elizabeth."

"Yeah?"

"Your body temperature has evened out enough."

"Good, I can take a nap then." I snuggled closer to him and tried to close my eyes. Strange, I did feel a lot better now. He pushed me forward and up so that I was standing in the tub.

"You can't go to sleep now. You need to get ready."

I put my hands to my chest, suddenly feeling very exposed. "For what?"

He stepped out of the tub to grab me a towel, studying my necklaces. I was glad I'd taken off my mother's. He wrapped the towel around my body and then he leaned over and pulled off his wet boxers. Instantly my body heated; he turned and I couldn't help but rake my eyes down his muscled and very naked body. I noticed he had several bite marks on his arms. Was that from the wolves?

"For your change."

I barely registered what he said but stepped forward to touch his arms. He didn't move but just watched me.

"Is this from earlier? Did my pack do this?"

He moved his head just enough for me to recognize it as an affirmative answer to my question. Then he grabbed another towel.

"You need to eat to get your strength back. Avery should've put some clothes in your room. Get dressed, then come to the kitchen."

He began to walk out of the bathroom while I checked out his perfectly shaped rear end, right before he wrapped his towel around it. Then what he said finally registered.

"Did you say I was going to change? What does that mean?"

He didn't answer me. Didn't even look back. What a jerk.

I sighed.

What a sexy jerk who saved my life.

&.

"FINE. DON'T ANSWER ME." I WAS GRUMBLING TO MYSELF AS I PUT MY mother's necklace back on because he was already gone. I grabbed the caddy and stacked the toilet paper rolls on the back of the toilet, taking the caddy with me. Hunter seemed okay; he could've easily done something to me in the bathtub if he'd wanted to. And hell, I may have let him, I was so turned on. I don't know what was wrong with me.

Must be the fever making me so hot.

Since he didn't do anything, I trusted him somewhat. But I wasn't so sure about anyone else.

I left the bathroom and tried to remember where my room was. I was in a hallway on the second floor; there was a bannister that over-looked the living room below. The room was really large with light that filtered through skylights onto large and comfortable looking sofas. I turned to the right, hoping this was the way towards my room.

The end of the hallway had huge glass sliding glass doors and I could see a large deck beyond it with no side rails. Hmmm. Convenient for dragons? I think so.

Good thing I wasn't afraid of heights.

I turned away from it to wander down the hallway, my towel -wrapped around my body with my clothes and the toilet paper caddy clasped to me tight. I had to look into three rooms before I found my own; they all seemed clean, expensively decorated and rarely used. The smell of bacon and eggs didn't help much except to distract me. I was ravenous.

Once I found a room that looked vaguely familiar, I closed the door behind me, leaned against it and closed my eyes. How had my world gone to shit in such a short time? My birthday party seemed a century ago.

Thanks for the fucking birthday present, Scarface.

I tried not to give in to the tightness in my chest, the darkness that threatened to overwhelm me, or the sobs that wanted to burst from me. I gripped the caddy so tight that it cut into my palm. I would kill Garrett as soon as I could shift. He would die at my own hands.

I took in a deep breath, trying to calm myself. One day at a time.

One hour, one minute, at a time.

I looked around the room. There was a dark walnut four-poster bed in the middle and on the drawers sat my gun and bag. I dropped the caddy and rushed to that side of the room. The bag was a bit muddy but the gun had been cleaned. I opened the bag to rummage through it. As far as I could tell, everything was still there. I touched the pencil topper and an ache throbbed in my chest; I wished that Aaron was with me now.

I dressed quickly, silently thanking whoever was in charge of getting me new clothes that they thought to buy a bra and some underwear. Red lace. Hmmm. Kinky.

Thank goodness they fit me, even if they were a little loose.

As soon as I was dressed, there was a knock at my door.

"Come in."

Avery peeked through the door, holding a tube and a small box in his hands. "Did you find the clothes?"

I nodded, suddenly feeling grateful for everything they'd done for me. "Thank you." It was all I could think of to say.

He shrugged, holding his hand to the back of his neck and staring at the floor. "It was nothing. Though I had to guess on your size." He'd looked up and noticed that I was staring at him with a strange look on my face and he frowned. "What?"

"I don't mean the clothes." I gestured towards the bag and gun. "For everything, I mean. You saved me, and I didn't even know that you guys existed. Why didn't my parents ever tell me?"

He sat on the bed and pat it. "Let me see your feet." Eyeing him warily but feeling better now that they'd brought me my gun, I sat next to him and put my right foot in his lap. He still didn't have a shirt on and I studied the tats curled around his finely shaped biceps. One of them was of a unicorn and I was tempted to ask him about it but decided against it.

"Your parents probably never told you because we don't tell anyone of our existence."

He unscrewed the lid to the tube and squeezed some gel onto his fingers. It smelled like an antiseptic. The gel stung but as he rubbed it in, the pain in my foot began to subside; his fingers were soft and his touch was soothing. I wondered what his fingers would feel like as they moved all over my body.

What the hell? I sharply rebuked myself. Something was seriously wrong with me. First Hunter and now Avery.

I tried to remember what we were talking about. "Why don't you show yourselves to the shifter world?"

"Because they would kill us if word got out that we existed." He didn't look at me as he spoke and his dark hair covered his brown eyes. I studied him. His olive-skinned body wasn't thick like Hunter but was lean and taut. He looked like a freaking greek god.

He gestured to my other foot and I switched legs.

"Who would?"

He looked up now, straight into my eyes. "The wolves."

My mouth dropped open. "No we wouldn't."

He was back to staring at my feet. "Yes, you would."

"I wouldn't!"

"Well, obviously. You're Robert's daughter. But the rest would."

"How can you say that?"

He stood up and I noticed that his burnt sienna-colored eyes had darkened. He put the lid on the tube of antiseptic and opened the box of Band-Aids. He smelled like the forest and it made me long for home.

"Were you the one who brought my things inside?"

He nodded. "I figured you would want them."

"I did, thanks."

Frowning, he sat back on the bed, brushing my ankles lightly with his fingers as he covered the soles of my feet in band aids. I swear he used the whole box and my feet felt sticky.

"Thanks."

He stood up. "You've already told me that."

I shrugged. "I am." We were silent for a moment and it bothered me that he hadn't answered my question. "Tell me, Avery. Why do you think that the wolves would kill you?"

He turned away from me to walk towards the door. "Because, that's what they've been doing for the past twenty years."

The room went silent as the shock of his words washed over me. Who was doing that? Was it anyone in *my* pack? And then another realization came over me. By saving me, they'd exposed themselves.

He reached the door. "Come on, you need to eat." He turned to look back at me, a puzzled look on his face. "Elizabeth? Why is the toilet paper caddy in here?"

❦

AVERY ROLLED HIS EYES AND THEN LEFT THE ROOM AFTER I JUST STARED at him stupidly, too embarrassed to answer. I put the bathroom caddy back then followed the smell of delicious food down the stairs and found the kitchen.

Hunter and Christian were talking and Christian laughed; it was light and easy and it made me smile a little.

Hunter leaned against the granite counter, a piece of crisp bacon to his mouth. I glanced at his full lips then looked away, pretending to check out the kitchen. It was large and open, with soft yellow walls that greeted me cheerfully. I tried not to notice how Hunter's eyes followed me as I passed the kitchen table. Christian had his back towards me and he was flipping pancakes on the griddle.

"Hi." I suddenly felt very shy.

Hunter raised his eyebrows at me without saying anything but Christian turned around. He was the only one wearing a shirt and it hugged his chest tightly.

"Hey! Glad to see you're out and about." He smiled, showing his perfect teeth. I also noticed a dimple on his right cheek. "Hungry?"

I nodded. "Like a bear looking for a campsite in the winter."

He grinned, then turned to put five perfectly round silver dollar sized pancakes on a plate. "Good thing I made plenty of food then."

He placed the plate filled with eggs, bacon and pancakes on the bar in front of me; it looked heavenly. The last person who had cooked for me was Aaron, who made the hash browns in a way that I could never imitate. Sadness weighed on my chest; Aaron may as well be on the other side of the world now. His dad would never let him leave willingly and besides, Aaron had to take care of his family. He would have to be strong for them and I would have to be strong for him.

I pushed him from my thoughts and forced myself to smile.

"I can get you some syrup..." Christian stared at me, his eyebrow raised as I began to devour the food in front of me.

"No need." I stopped eating just enough to say this in between bites. "Don't need it." Hell, I was being rude. "Thank you for the food. And the saving my life and all that." And for all of you being so damn sexy, I added in my head. Makes for nice eye candy while my world burns to hell.

"Sure." Christian smiled but Hunter just grunted in response. After Christian handed Hunter a plate piled with food, he moved to sit next to me at the bar.

Avery entered the room. "Got any for me?"

Hunter seemed to sit closer to me than was necessary and it made me very aware of my own body. His arm rubbed against mine as he reached for the syrup and the hair on my arm tingled.

Avery sat next to Hunter, and Christian piled several pancakes on his plate. Avery reached across Hunter and grabbed the syrup out of his hands, just as Hunter was about to pour it.

"What the hell, dude?"

Avery's eyebrow went up. "Did you just call me dude?" Christian put the plate down in front of him and Avery poured the syrup on his pancakes.

"Dude, nerd, asshole..."

Avery put the syrup on the other side of his plate, away from Hunter. "Everybody knows that you take all of the syrup. I'd say that would make you the asshole in this room." He shoved a triangle of pancakes in his mouth.

Hunter reached over his plate, intentionally shoving his elbow into Avery's hand which made him get syrup all over his face. "Since this is your second breakfast and the syrup is halfway gone already, you seem to be more like the syrup hogger."

Christian sniggered as he rinsed out the batter bowl.

Avery looked at Christian, grabbing a napkin off the table to wipe his face. "You ate at the same time as me, brother."

Christian pulled the muzzle from the sink out and sent a shower of water in Avery's direction. "I didn't even eat any pancakes, syrup hogger."

"Hey!" Avery jumped back, then he ran for Christian who moved the muzzle to spray Avery directly in the face.

"Liar!" The whole kitchen was sprinkled in a mist of water as Avery wrestled Christian for control over the muzzle. I laughed, forgetting my problems for a moment. Hunter stuck his fork in his pancakes, watching them blandly, clearly used to this kind of behavior. Avery managed to get control and soon Christian was drenched. He put his palm in front of it, spraying the water back onto Avery who reacted by moving it higher.

Christian batted the muzzle with his hand, hitting it into the sink, then jumped on Avery's back and went down on the floor. Hunter looked at me, smirking.

"Looks like the masculinity show is on in full force."

I put my hand in my cup, and sprinkled water on Hunter. "Only guys act that way, is that right?"

He froze, his fork halfway to his mouth and growled. Then he got up and stepped over them; they were now wrestling on the ground, with Christian currently on top. Hunter grabbed the nozzle and turned it towards me, a mischievous grin on his face.

I threw my hands up in the air. "Okay, okay!" He gave me a quick spurt that landed in my face.

I shrieked and, as I wiped at my face, he offered me a hand towel. While I dried my face he sat back next to me.

I was tempted to throw my glass of water on him. Instead, I threw the towel at him, smiling. "Not fair."

He caught it and placed it on the table, then began to eat again. "I know." He nodded towards the guys. "They haven't acted like this since Sophia." He raised his eyebrow. "Actually, that's not true. Avery never acts this way."

I ate slowly, trying to absorb what he was telling me. "Who's Sophia?"

He looked at me and frowned. "Someone you never want to meet."

"Why's that?"

"Cuz she's a bitch. That's why."

"Oh." I wasn't sure where to go with that.

Christian and Avery were now both lying in a puddle of water on the ground, breathing heavily. Christian stood up, pulling Avery with him and looking at me.

"I know, let's have the new girl tell us who the syrup hog is." He winked at me. "Take a guess." He tried to be sly about pointing to Avery but Avery shoved his hand away.

"I don't need Elizabeth to tell me that you're the syrup hog." He went back to his seat, frowning. Christian laughed and Avery growled at him. "Shut up, man."

Christian turned from him and pulled a zillion paper towels off the rack and began to clean up the water. Hunter leaned closer to me and my breathing hitched at his closeness. "Psst, I'll give you a hint." Then he pointed towards Avery.

Avery shot out of his seat and took his plate, only halfway done with his pancakes, and threw it into the sink with a clatter. "I'm going out."

Hunter called out to Avery, who reached the door. "Check the perimeter since some of the cameras aren't working."

"Duh." Avery swiveled out the screen door, slamming it behind him.

"Is he always so charming?" I was scraping the last bit of food off my plate.

Hunter, who'd filled his mouth with his next bite, just shrugged but Christian looked towards the door. "This is him on a good day."

I glanced towards the door again. Avery had stripped off all of his clothes and was jogging towards the woods.

"Is he going to shift?"

"Yeah." Christian grabbed the last piece of bacon off of Hunter's plate, who stopped eating to give him a deathly glare. Christian quickly shoved it into his mouth. Silence stretched between us as Christian swallowed it in two bites and I studied Hunter out of the corner of my eye. The side of his lips tugged upwards even though he was still giving Christian his best 'eat shit' look.

Ignoring him, Christian looked at me. "He's the smallest dragon of the three of us and he can fly low enough to remain undetected. He'll catch anyone approaching."

"How long was I asleep?" Now that I had some food in my stomach, I felt a dreamy sensation wash over me.

"Long enough to get your energy back. You're going to need it." Hunter's fingers brushed over my knee as he got up to wash his plate. I hopped up to help clean the kitchen; it was the least I could do.

I filled the sink with soapy water and tackled the plates next to the sink while Hunter stood beside me to rinse and dry. He was standing so close to me that it awakened my wolf. I had the sudden desire to grab his hips and yank him to me, just to see what his reaction would be. Would he kiss me if I did that?

I frowned and pushed my wolf down, thinking of Aaron. "Why?"

"You're going to shift soon."

I stopped washing the dish in my hands and swallowed hard, then looked at him. "How do you know?"

Christian gathered the pans off the stove and put them next to the plates. "You have the signs. Tiredness, fever."

"Hunger." Hunter looked at my mouth and I realized I had some butter smeared on my lips. I wiped it off and he watched me intently. I had a sudden vision of him sucking the butter off my lips and warmth shot through my chest.

I cleared my throat, hoping the burning in my cheeks wasn't

obvious and telling my wolf to freaking calm down. "Wolves don't get fevers before we shift. And I'm always tired and hungry. Plus, I could be tired because..." I thought of my dead parents. I looked at Christian, hoping that Hunter didn't notice the tremble of my lips. "Are you sure?"

He looked at Hunter, who raised his shoulders. "Maybe. I guess we'll see. But it would be nice if you could. Otherwise, we'll have to stick to the car."

"Couldn't I just..." I thought of how thrilling it would be to fly through the air. "Could I ride on one your backs?"

Hunter rolled his eyes and a burst of laughter came from Christian. Hunter took the last plate from my hands. "No, you cannot just ride on our backs. We aren't your pet."

Wow. Talk about a reaction. "Sorry, I didn't realize."

"Not yet, anyway." Christian put a pan in the water and then stood behind me, pushing against my back and pressing his mouth at my ear. "I wouldn't mind it if you rode me." A shiver went down my back.

Hunter bumped into him as he put away the stack of plates, shoving him off me. "Shut up, Christian. No one is riding anyone."

Christian just smirked at me, then he pulled the washrag through my hands and went to wash down the bar. I studied the way his body moved for a minute before I realized that Hunter was watching me. I grabbed my water glass, the only thing unwashed, and took a swallow.

"So now what?"

Hunter dried the last pan. "We keep you safe here. And when we know it's okay to leave, we take you home."

I stared at him. "Your home?" I took another swallow.

He nodded. "A safe place, at least."

Of course. Where else? We weren't going back to my parents' house.

"And then what?"

He looked at me, his eyes smoldering. "And then we decide what to do with you."

A heat rose in my chest and I chugged down the rest of my water as images of what he *could* do to me ran through my head. I needed to take a chill pill and regroup. I had to find out how I could get to Aaron, not dream about what kinds of sexy things Hunter could be doing to me. Furious with myself for even forgetting things for a moment, I ran my finger over the top of the glass angrily.

I had to fix everything. I had to figure out how to shift and then go back and challenge that asshole, Scarface. I thought about my own home and choked on the last of the water in my mouth. Oh hell, I hadn't called into work.

"Can I use your phone? I need to call into work."

When Hunter frowned, his lips pressed together tightly. "You can't. It's not safe, your pack is probably tracking your work line."

"Sorry, sweetie." Christian called from across the kitchen; he was staring into the fridge and I wondered if he was going to eat again or if he was just planning for lunch.

I crossed my arms and leaned back against the counter again, putting my glass on it. I sighed. He was right, of course. I'd taken a couple days off at the mortgage company to deal with pack issues but my boss was going to worry if I didn't come in soon. That or kill me for leaving my clients in the middle of their house buying process.

There was a scratch at the back porch door and Hunter jumped, pushing me behind him. Christian silently closed the fridge door and pulled a pocket knife from his jeans and crept forward. Hunter's hand was pressing me closer into his back and I could feel my heart pick up. Crap. Why did he have such a crazy effect on my body? It was like my body instinctively knew he was mine. I felt something stir inside of me: the magic of my wolf. I was tempted to nip at his shoulder.

We couldn't see anyone through the screen door but the scratching grew louder.

As soon as Christian reached it, he visibly relaxed and folded his knife. "It's a kitten." He opened the door and an adorable little face peeked into the kitchen. "I think it's a stray."

"Awe." I moved out of Hunter's reach to go to the kitten. "A hungry little stray." The grey and white kitten was very thin and dirty. And could possibly have fleas.

I bent down, letting him? Her? Her. Check me out. Cats don't usually like wolves. The cat looked up at me with big soft eyes and then rubbed his head against my leg.

"Want some milk, kitty?" Christian opened a cupboard to grab a bowl.

I picked up the kitten and took her to the fridge to look for milk. Hunter sighed but didn't say anything.

As soon as I grabbed the milk a deep pain shot up my back. I cried out, dropping both the milk and the cat. The kitten shot to the living room to hide under the couch. I fell to the floor; the pain was shooting through my whole body now and I grit my teeth, trying not to cry. There was a clawing in my stomach, ripping and shredding my insides, like a wild beast trying to get out.

5

J screamed as another wave of pain enveloped my body. I folded myself into the fetal position, clutching at my stomach. Then Hunter picked me up and took me to the couch, cradling me in his arms. I closed my eyes, gritting my teeth against the pain.

A sharp shooting pain ran across my face, digging into my eyes and making me clench my jaw. I rubbed at my face, wishing I could rip it off. The agony was so intense, I was beginning to feel faint.

Hunter's cool fingers ran over my forehead and the pain lessened. I pressed my head into his chest, moving it back and forth, trying to rub the throbbing ache that ran down my body away. Hunter's fingers moved over my arms, my stomach, my thighs. With every touch, the agony bled out of my body until it was only a warm burning.

I closed my eyes, feeling drained and he ran his hands through my hair, whispering comforting words in my ears.

"You're going to turn soon, and then you'll be glorious and powerful."

I lay against him limply, all my energy spent.

His hands continued to caress my arm and I felt a blanket cover me. I opened my eyes to look at Christian, who was looking down at me with troubled green eyes. He bit his lip and I reached up towards him.

He knelt next to me and I touched his cheek and smiled weakly, grateful for the blanket. Then I snuggled deeper into Hunter's chest. He began to hum and the deep rumbling in his chest created a calm that washed over me like a child's lullaby.

The front door opened and Christian jumped up. "Easton. I didn't know you were coming."

I turned to look at the newcomer. Easton. They'd said his name before - he was the one watching the trackers on my pack. He marched towards us, straight-backed and stiff. His short, dark, brown hair matched his eyes and they were taking me in, then they moved back to Christian.

"I took the plane. I'm here to get you guys out. You've been compromised."

Christian moved to stand behind the couch. "She can't leave yet, she's undergoing the change."

Easton paused for a moment, considering me. "She's going to have to deal with it. We have a small window before they'll find this place. I've got the pilot on standby."

Hunter gripped me tighter, growling. "Didn't you hear Christian? She's undergoing the change. Who knows what could happen? And I'd rather not find out what her magic can do to a tin can in the middle of the sky."

Easton leaned over to meet Hunter's eyes, scowling. "You're the one who needs to get his hearing checked. I told you. You've been compromised. You need to get out. Now. Or they'll find you. Garrett has a few hundred of the pack in on this; we're no match for them."

"And what if her magic blows up the plane? I'd rather take my chances with the pack." Hunter looked down at me. "Elizabeth, do you think you can force the change now?"

Easton growled, leaning over me to shove his face into Hunter's. "That's not going to help. She won't be able to just do it because we want her to, and we need to leave. Now."

Hunter met his stare and by his look I wondered if he was going to toss me aside and get in a brawling match with Easton right here in the living room.

"I can try." My voice was so small compared to the large personalities in the room but I had to try. I was putting them in danger and maybe I also wanted to show Easton that I could do it. If I was petty like that.

I moved to drop out of Hunter's arms but he leaned over to gently place me on the ground. I kneeled over so that I was on all fours, feeling absolutely ridiculous and wishing that I'd paid better attention in the shifter classes. Oh wait, we didn't have those.

With all eyes on me, I closed my eyes and tried to shift.

Nothing.

I concentrated all my thoughts on shifting and even imagined a large wolf that looked a lot like Aaron. Hey, anything to help a gal out right? I felt a small rumble in my chest and focused all my attention on that. As soon as I focused on it, it slipped away. Dangit!

I peeked one eye open to see a half smirk on Hunter's face. Easton was frowning and Christian was looking positively empathetic.

I focused on Christian. "Got any pointers?"

He looked at the other guys then sat down to be at eye level with me, biting his lip. "Well, it works differently for different people, but for me it helps to clear my mind. Kind of like what you would do when you meditate."

I raised one eyebrow. "Meditate?" I didn't take Christian for one of those kinds of people.

"Yeah." He sat down all the way and crossed his legs. "Sit like this."

I glanced up to the other guys but they just looked like they were trying to be very patient. So I sat down on my butt and crossed my legs. He scooted up so that our knees were touching and he put the back of his hands on my legs. "Touch me. Put your hands over mine."

I did it.

"Now close your eyes."

Easton sighed loudly. "Christian, we don't have time for this."

I looked up but Christian took my chin and forced me to look into his eyes. "Ignore him. Just focus on me."

As soon as I held his stare, I felt myself drawn to him and I couldn't look away. All of my thoughts and worries fell away. My body loosened and I felt the stress from the past couple of days drain away. My shoulders, which had been tightly wound, relaxed and even my hands felt lazy. My eyes began to close.

"That's it." Christian's voice sounded so far away. "Now, imagine you're in the woods."

Instantly my body reacted and I seized up, remembering the last time I was in the woods behind my house.

"Sorry, forget that. Just take a deep breath in."

The trees were flying past me. I heard my ragged breath, my hand clutched tightly to my gun. Then the blood was spraying on the tv, the dead shifter slumped over on the couch.

"Elizabeth! Stop."

I opened my eyes and could see my own fear reflected in his eyes. My heart was pounding in my chest.

"I'm sorry, that was my fault. Keep your eyes open for a moment and focus on me."

I stared into his eyes again and felt myself slipping back into a relaxed state. My heartbeat slowed and Christian squeezed my hands gently.

"Now close your eyes and imagine yourself in a hammock, on the beach."

I saw my toes as they swung back and forth as the white sand stretched before me.

"How is the water? Is it blue and clear? Or is it deep?"

"It's crystal clear. I can see my feet through the water."

"Good. Now imagine yourself turning into a wolf."

Instead of facing the vastness of the ocean, I faced the shore and imagined a pathway through the tropical forest beyond it. I began to run, and the feel of the wind over my skin rushed through me.

"It's not working. If she doesn't change soon, we'll have to go. We can't wait for her to do it." Easton's voice interrupted my flow and I tripped over a rock. I flew to the ground, scraping my arms.

"Shhh…" Christian's soothing voice was in my thoughts. "Ignore him, block him totally out."

I put up a mental wall. "Now, get up."

I stood up, wincing as I brushed the sand off my arms. "Forget about that, it's gone now."

And it was. Well holy hell. I suddenly realized that he could see inside my mind. I opened my eyes, alarmed. His eyes were staring into me. Not into my eyes, but into *me*. We were alone, no longer in the room but alone together on the beach.

"I'm not going to hurt you. I'm only trying to help."

I hesitated for a moment, considering him.

"I'll stop if you want. You control this, Elizabeth."

I nodded.

"Do you want me to?"

I shook my head. "No, it's okay. It's just… I'm a little afraid is all." I swallowed hard, my first time ever admitting to anyone except Aaron that I was scared.

His eyes softened. "I understand. I was nervous the first time I shifted. And you can't even imagine your arms becoming these humongous wings!"

I grinned, considering it. He was right. I nodded again. "I'm alright. I can do this."

He nodded. "Okay, close your eyes then."

I did it and felt the ocean breeze on my face.

His voice entered my thoughts. "Now, see the path again. And run."

I ran. And it was exhilarating. I ran faster than I'd ever run before, the sand spraying behind me as my feet moved over it.

"Now shift."

I imagined my feet turning into wolf legs and hair growing on my arms.

"Don't imagine yourself shifting. Just do it."

I held my breath, waiting for it to happen and just explode from me. Nothing.

Easton sighed.

I opened my eyes; we were back in the living room. Even Hunter looked disappointed and the weight of it crushed me.

Easton stood up. "Where's Avery? We need to go."

Hunter stood up to face Easton. "I told you, we're not leaving. She could change at any moment and I'm not going to risk it."

Easton's face turned red. "You may be in charge of these two dragons, but when I'm around, you're not the Alpha."

"No one is the Alpha of our Clan, it hasn't been established yet." He grit his teeth and his hands were clenched at his side. "But when we're out in the field, I'm in charge of getting us to safety, and I say we can't trust her shifting on the plane. Or in the middle of the road either."

The blood rushed to my head and an intense pressure threatened to bust from inside me. Was I really such a threat? In such a few short days I'd become the angel of death; marked to kill any who tried to help me.

The desire to run away washed over me, to leave them and to sacrifice myself to the woods to save whatever lives could be saved. I couldn't risk my pack getting ahold of them; I'd already put them in enough danger. I also couldn't risk blowing up innocent lives on a plane or anywhere else.

I needed to go.

Easton was inches from Hunter now. "You may think you're the big kahuna out in the field, but you haven't seen what I've seen back in headquarters. They're onto us and if we want to make it out alive, we need to go now."

Christian moved to stand in between the two men, pushing the palm of his hands against their chests. "You guys aren't helping any! She's freaking out over there."

All three men turned towards me and the pressure of their stare was too overwhelming. I turned to run out the door and just as I opened it, I crashed into Avery, who was just coming in.

His arms enveloped me as we crashed back into the door.

I could sense his fear. "What is it? Tell me."

"Your pack... they're everywhere. I tried to fly back as soon as I found them all. They have us surrounded. They'll be here in five minutes."

✌

I STARED AT AVERY, MY MOUTH OPEN IN SHOCK. "HOW DID THEY FIND us here?"

Hunter jumped to his feet and left for the back room.

Easton walked over to the window, his hands behind his straight back. "I told you, they tracked us to these mountains. It was only a matter of time before they found our house."

"Is there a red-haired wolf with them?" I climbed off Avery and held out my hand to help him off the door.

Avery shook his head, grasping my hand and pulled himself forward. "There's too many of them to tell, but they are being led by a silvery golden one."

I bit my lip. "Shayne. He's the best tracker of the pack. Why would he do this? I thought he was loyal to my dad."

Christian touched my arm and it was soothing. "He doesn't have a choice. Every wolf in the pack has to follow the Alpha."

Easton stared out the window. "You should know that already."

"I thought I understood, but how could Garrett kill my dad then? If he couldn't disobey him?"

"The wolf can't disobey a direct order but once an Alpha is challenged, all bets are off."

I thought about what happened that night. As soon as Garrett came into the house, he'd yelled out the challenge. So my dad couldn't order him to leave. I clenched my hands in fury. What a freaking coward.

And now, was he even here? He was a large wolf, Avery probably would've noticed him. He should be leading the pack, not Shayne. Especially if Shayne was tracking me under duress. Now what? Would I have to fight with them? And kill them? Even if they were fighting me against their own wishes.

And I still couldn't shift!

Ugh!

I paced the floor and Christian's eyes followed me. Hunter came back into the room with several rifles. He strode directly towards me and my heart raced as he neared me. He put my gun in my hands, along with my bag. "You need to leave. We'll stay here so they'll think you're with us. Take Avery's bike."

"No way." I wasn't going to put them all in danger and just run away.

Avery was back with a pair of jeans on. He pressed his keys into my hand, his serious eyes gazing into mine. "You need to leave." Then he pressed his lips to my forehead and Hunter looked away quickly. Easton walked up to Hunter, holding out his hand. "Here, I'll help you set these up."

Hunter passed one of the rifles over along with a box of ammo.

I gripped Avery's keys tight. "I'm *not* leaving."

Christian turned me to look at him. "Please, Elizabeth. We can take care of ourselves."

I frowned. "Of course I know that."

"Then why won't you leave? Do you want one of us to go with you?" His green eyes studied mine.

"No, I don't need one of you with me. I'm going to stay." Easton sighed and I felt the weight of their words press into me. "I'm not going."

Hunter set down his rifle and picked up another one. "Lizabeth." His voice was low, a warning. He was used to people following his orders.

Well, so was I.

I threw the keys to the ground, feeling childish but I couldn't help it. "I'm not leaving, okay?"

He frowned and gripped the butt of the rifle. The scope gleamed in the light.

Suddenly, Avery was in front of me again and I felt an instant pull to him. I looked into his eyes as his hands touched my shoulders, then moved down my arms. His fingers felt soft, nimble and as they moved over me, I knew that he was exploring more than my body. I couldn't move or turn my attention to any of the other guys; I was frozen in time, my attention completely on him.

His hands moved up my neck and he gripped the side of my face and pulled me closer. A spark of electricity flickered between us and the hair on my arms and the back of my neck rose. My lips parted and I let out a breath. He leaned forward so that he was only inches from me and then he was breathing me into him. He was inside my mind and I was falling, falling into a dark abyss.

And then he stepped back and let me go and I snapped back to the present.

"What was that?"

He turned towards Hunter. "Let her stay."

Hunter frowned. "Why?"

"Because she feels guilty that she couldn't help her parents; they locked her in a safe room and she couldn't do anything. She felt helpless as they killed her parents, and doesn't want to feel that way again."

Hunter sighed. "Fine."

"Hey!" I folded my arms. "That's my private business. And how did you know that?"

It was true. I didn't even know it until he said it, but as soon as the words were out of his mouth, I knew that he'd seen something inside me. I was naked before him and he saw me as I was.

Christian picked up one of the guns and handed it to me, his eyebrow raised and a half smile on his face. "Looks like you're staying."

"Absolutely not. She'll just be a liability." Easton had disappeared from the room and now he reappeared with a bag and he shoved it into my hands. "There's another home we can send you to, another safe house we have. They'll never find you there. Here's the rest of the clothes that Avery bought you and I've included the address to that home. Leave here now and we'll meet you there in three days."

Hunter moved towards him. "She's staying with us. Besides, I thought we gave out that address to no one."

"Edward gave me permission."

I threw the bag down, furious. They may have saved my life back in the woods, but that didn't give them permission to dictate the rest of my life. I was the fucking Fated Alpha and I would make decisions for my own life from here on out.

My dad was dead and I was the Alpha now, even if it was of a pack of one: me.

I faced Easton and stared him in the eyes, a challenge. "I'm not leaving you here while you guys play bait. I will not run away like a scared little puppy. I know the pack better than you, and I'm pretty handy with a gun. Besides, I don't want to kill my pack if I can help it. Maybe we can think of a way to escape without harming them."

His eyes met my challenge and we stared each other down. "You can't even shift. You'll be a liability, and you'll get my guys hurt."

I took a step forward. "I'm *not* leaving."

After what felt like a forever staring match, Easton looked away to mumble under his breath. "Fine."

I touched his arm. "I promise you that I will protect you guys, as you have protected me."

He nodded, satisfied, then moved towards the stairs. "I'll check the cameras, try to see if I can get a view of their direction and numbers."

Hunter didn't say anything but just raised his eyebrow towards me, then gave me a box of bullets. I nodded my head and he moved towards the window.

I went to Avery who was about to leave to do a final assessment. He had his shirt off already and I put my hand on his arm to keep him from leaving.

"How did you know that? What did you do to me?"

He shrugged and put his hand on mine. "I just know things some-times." Then he peeled my hand off his arm and opened the door to leave.

I grunted. "Just don't do that again. Or I'll cut your bloody balls off."

His eyes widened for a moment and then he was out the door.

❧

Avery was outside for only a second, then he rushed back in through the door. He gripped my hand as he ran through it, jerking me inside the kitchen and then pushed me to the floor. Glass exploded around us and he covered me with his body. Shards flew through the air, piercing his back and my exposed arms.

An intense heat roared through the room as fire exploded in the room, spreading through the kitchen and setting it on fire. As soon as the glass settled on the floor, we were up and running into the living room.

Easton ran down the stairs, staring at Christian who was using the faucet from the kitchen sink to spray down the fire but it wasn't helping much. "They've surrounded the house, they're just behind the tree line."

Hunter ran into the bathroom and came out with an armful of wet towels, trying to smother the fire with them but it was quickly getting out of control and spreading into the other rooms.

Easton ran through the fire, catching his shirt on fire. He yanked it over his head and stomped on it, then opened the cupboard under the sink and pulled out a fire extinguisher. Working quickly, he began to spray the fire.

Avery tried to run towards the kitchen to help but I I grabbed his hand, forcing him to stay. "I need to fix this, stay here."

Large chunks of glass were poking out of his back, including one that was in pretty deep. Blood was running down his back, staining his pants and I knew he needed to get the glass out in order heal.

"But I need to help—"

"If I don't fix this, then you're going to bleed out. Or you could get an infection."

The room was getting really hot and smoky. "Do you have a butterfly Band-Aid? Or maybe some duct tape? That would be better."

He nodded and pointed to the closet near the front door.

"Stay here." I used my most commanding voice, then ran to the closet. I rummaged through it and finally found some duct tape. I went back to him, coughing. I pulled out the big piece of glass first and blood came gushing out. I yanked off my shirt and pressed it to his back. Then gently but quickly, took out the rest of the smaller pieces in his back and taped the shirt over the cuts. He was going to kill me when I had to take that off of him.

As soon as I was done, the window next to me exploded and I threw my hands over my head. The front door opened and another firebomb was thrown in. Avery grabbed my waist and pulled me forward while the living room exploded in light and smoke.

The fire raged from both sides of the house now and the fire extinguisher was empty. I stared at Avery, unable to hide the fear in my eyes. He pulled me forward. "It's okay. We'll get out of this."

Holding my hand, he pulled me towards the stairs. "Up guys, this floor is about to go up in flames."

Hunter grunted his agreement and Avery led all of us up the stairs.

Panic began to crawl up my throat and the helplessness of my situation began to wash over me. It was just like before. We were unprepared for their viciousness and it was going to kill us. "How are we going to get out of the house if the whole bottom floor is on fire?"

We were running through the hallway to the master bedroom and suddenly I remembered the cat. I yanked my hand from Avery's and pushed away the rest of the guys, who fell like pins because they were so surprised by my action. As I flew down the stairs, all four men followed me back down the stairs, yelling at me, asking me what the hell I was doing.

Heat threatened to engulf me as I landed on the bottom floor. I threw myself to the ground as sweat ran down my face and back. I put my face to the floor, trying to breathe as little as possible as I crawled on the floor towards the couch.

Flaming bits of ash floated in the air and my hair singed on the ends. I coughed as smoke filled my lungs but I pushed forward until I reached the couch. I put my hand under it, searching for the kitten, only to be rewarded by a long scratch up my arm.

"Come on cat. Help me out here." I gripped her by the neck and dragged her out from under the sofa. As soon as she was cradled in the crook of my arm, a pair of arms clamped around my waist and pulled me back towards the stairs. Hunter.

The heat singed my back and I knew I was going to have at least second degree burns. Then we were flying across the room so fast that I closed my eyes and allowed Hunter to lead me back towards the stairs.

I hoped there was a fire escape up there because we were in a crapload of trouble down here. When we reached the top of the landing, a pain shot up my back and I fell forward, cradling my hands around the cat to protect her.

I cried out as the pain shot through my whole body and I knew in that moment that I was going to break my word to Easton because I couldn't move, I could barely breathe, and I was putting everyone else in danger.

6

The pain intensified up my back and spread throughout my arms and legs. I couldn't press forward, even though the intensity from the fire was beginning to burn my legs. Thick, black smoke pressed into the stairwell and into the ceiling.

My lungs felt frozen; I could barely manage small sips of air because anything deeper would cause a shooting pain in my chest. Then a splintering pain shot up from my arm and the bones in my wrist began to shift. Popping bones slid up my arm as my bones in both arms broke.

"No!" I cried out as tears fell down my face, the smoke in the air making them burn. The cat clung to my chest and I tried not to put all of my weight on her. I wish she'd just run off to safety but her claws dug into my skin, clinging to me as much as I was clinging on to my sanity.

Hunter knelt and gathered me in his arms, yelling at Avery. "Shift so you can protect her from the fire."

Feet shuffled around me but I couldn't move my head to see what the guys were doing. Then a pair of jeans fell to the ground to pool around a set of legs.

The pain in my hands moved into my chest and I felt like my whole body was tearing apart. I needed to shift, or I would die right here and now in this blazing house. I closed my eyes, trying to push all the pain out of my mind. My chest burned, my legs burned, I was boiling alive.

I grit my teeth and pushed away everything. All thought. All the pain. My mind was blank, I was enveloped in darkness.

Christian and Easton surrounded me and as Avery moved his wings to stretch across my body I felt the scorching heat subside. Hunter was running his hand through my hair, humming that damn song. I tried to shift again, focusing all my energy on the thought.

I had to do it! It was the only way to survive this. I willed it.

But nothing happened.

I thought of Scarface, his ruthlessness in killing my mom. She was helpless in the face of so many wolves. I wanted to rip my heart out of my chest to stop the searing pain from their absence. I wondered at all the betrayal and agony in the world. Maybe I would be better off passing on from this life, then I wouldn't have to suffer through all this pain.

Wouldn't it just be easier if I just died? Then the dragons could escape through the windows and fly away, without having to save my sorry ass.

Aaron could focus on saving his family; if I was dead, he could see himself as the Fated Alpha. He would grow strong enough to save himself and his family.

And maybe I could see my parents again.

That thought made me freeze. They'd sacrificed their life to give me mine.

Wasn't that worth something?

My cat rubbed her ragged head across my chest and I briefly rubbed between her ears as she purred. Clutching her, my fingers brushed over the plastic necklace at my throat. What about Carrie and her family? Would Garrett take care of them as my mother had? Did he always take care of pack?

I thought of the new shifter; the black wolf and something told me he was trouble. He'd aided in the death of my dad; an illegal fight for Alpha. Someone like that wouldn't care about the rest of the pack.

I gripped the necklace tight.

Was Aaron really strong enough to save the pack? Would the pack see him as an Alpha?

Garrett had muzzled him in front of the pack. That kind of shame was hard to forget. They may never see him as the Alpha.

There was no one else strong enough, no one else in line as Alpha.

I had to save them. Because no one else would do it.

The pack needed me and I was going to kick that asshole's ass.

I squeezed my eyes tighter and instead of allowing a void to come over all of my thoughts, I channeled all of my anger instead. He'd killed my parents.

He'd forced the pack to follow him.

He'd betrayed them by bringing in another Alpha to fight my dad.

He tried to kill me.

Now he would pay.

I'm not weak and I'm not afraid. Not anymore.

I was going to save my pack and kill the man who murdered my family.

All of my anger built up inside and my mother's necklace began to burn. A ball of rage twisted in my chest, pushing the insides of my rib cage, ready to burst out. I screamed, the pressure too great, and a blaze of blue light burst from the necklace.

The energy flew from the necklace through my body and into the men now surrounding me. As it enveloped their bodies, my body gave in to the power threatening to blow my body to bits. Bright white fur erupted on my hands, growing as it moved up my hands and feet. I was a white wolf, *just like my dad.*

Hunter scrambled out of reach to give me room as my bones cracked and shifted. I cried out in pain as the animal inside me clawed it's way out. I grew several feet; I was almost as large as Avery. Finally my wolf's energy burst out and I completed the shift.

A burning sensation moved through my body as the magic from

the necklace flowed between us, sealing the bond between the dragons and me.

{{·}}

As soon as the magic subsided, Easton fell to his knees. "What the hell just happened?"

I stayed in my wolf form and, grabbing the kitten by the scruff of its neck with my teeth, I passed it off to Christian. Then I slinked down the stairs.

The magic from my shift snuffed out the fire and now the downstairs was just smoke and ash.

"Elizabeth!" Christian called after me, but I ignored him.

I was going to stop this once and for all. It was my life they wanted, my head on a platter and I was going to protect us or die in the process.

Hunter leapt off the stairwell to land gracefully next to me. He grabbed ahold of the fur above my neck and I turned to snap my deadly teeth at him. He yanked his arm back but moved to stand in front of me. The rest of the guys were clomping down the landing.

Hunter stood his ground. "`Elizabeth, we're not letting you go out there alone. They'll kill you easily."

I growled, a warning low in my throat. Get out of my way. I shoved him to the side with my muzzle and he stumbled back.

Suddenly he was yanking down his pants and his shift moved over him like rippling magic; I stared in awe at the beauty of his shift. His wings were too big for the house and they crashed through the rooms, knocking over everything as he situated himself to face me. He flapped his wings aggressively and I noted the shimmering blue of his scaled skin as it wrapped around his impressive muscles; he was a force of nature. Then he moved towards me and lowered his head.

Princess. Even in my head I could hear his sarcasm. *You're not going out there alone. We are not helpless. We can protect each other.*

I don't want them to die. Not if they don't have to.

The rest of the guys crowded around me, Avery still in his dragon form but Christian and Easton hadn't shifted yet. I imagined if they did the whole house might explode; there wasn't enough room.

I turned towards them. *They're my pack, even if I'm not their Alpha right now. I'm their rightful ruler and I'll do anything to protect them. Even if they're trying to kill me.*

Easton moved to look out the window but Christian touched my fur. "There are two packs, right?"

I turned my head. *Explain.*

"When we were looking for you, there were two groups of wolves colored golden and grey. Your pack is golden?"

I shook my head. *Yes.*

Avery intervened. *The packs are still divided. I saw that when I was doing reconnaissance. Your pack is to the north and east of the house. The other pack is south and west.*

I nodded, thinking of the way the black wolf tore my dad apart. *Then we go for the other pack. Kill them if needed.*

Easton gestured his hand towards the guys. "We go out the back door, towards the new pack to create a distraction." He looked at me, sensing my growing anger that he was excluding me from this. "You said that your tracker was loyal to your dad?"

I nodded.

"Do you think he could turn again? If you dominate him, would he serve you? And be your spy?"

I mulled this over. I'd never fought before and Shayne was a strong wolf. But if he didn't want to serve shithead Scarface, then he may acquiesce easily. I would be taking a risk but it may work.

Easton continued. "We attack the new pack and you go after your tracker. If you win, then you turn him and escape through the woods. Follow the road east until you find a small airport, about ten miles out. Your tracker can help you if you need it. Our main goal is to get out of here alive."

I growled. I wanted the new pack dead. They'd help kill my father and take over my pack.

Easton looked into my wolf eyes. "For now. You need training, to learn how to shift on command. How to fight without killing and how to fight the Alpha. When you're ready, you'll come back and challenge him."

Everyone turned to me, waiting to see what I would say.

It seemed like a solid plan to me. Why the hell not? If my pack tore me apart then at least I'd tried.

I nodded my head.

§.

I WONDERED HOW HUNTER WOULD GET OUT OF THE HOUSE BUT HE SHOT through the air, ripping half of the roof off. Avery followed him and shingles and drywall came crashing down around us.

Easton and Christian told me how to get to the main road that led to the meeting point. Then they ran towards the back door and, after Christian put the cat down, shooing her towards the woods, they slipped out and disappeared in the darkness.

Instead of heading outside, I moved inwards towards the bathroom. Creeping slowly on the cold marble floor, I headed towards the window to look outside. My wolf eyes could see deep into the forest where I saw many wolves that I recognized.

A low growl rose in my throat.

Light flashed at the corner of my vision and I knew that the dragons were providing the distraction that I needed. Many of the shifters ran towards the light and it was then that I saw Shayne. His silver fur stood out among the dark woods and he didn't run towards the light - instead, his eyes searched the woods. Looking for me, I presumed.

Shayne was always the smart one. He used to help my dad fix old clocks that my dad insisted were antiques. Shayne was always the one who found the impossible parts and figured out how to make them work.

I slunk out of the bathroom and waited until the rest of my pack had followed the dragons. Then I burst out of the front door and sprinted towards him. He saw me as soon as I left the house and he lowered himself on his haunches, baring his teeth at me.

My long legs made the distance short and I barreled into him, aiming for his throat. He reared up on top of me for a brief moment and then he fell to his side, his feet slipping on the leaves and pine straw. He recovered quickly, jumping up to snap at my muzzle. He managed to grip his jaws around it and he bit into it hard.

Yelping, I remembered barging into my dad's office, crying because I'd scraped my knees roller skating. Shayne and my dad were studying a clock and the table next to them was littered with little pieces of metal.

I pushed forward, I was at least thirty pounds heavier than him, making him stumble backwards. Digging in, he lost his grip on my muzzle and I pushed harder, finally forcing him on his back. I barred my teeth at him, a warning growl. *Stop Shayne. I will show you mercy if you give in now.* My energy pounded into him as my Alpha magic came alive.

I put my front paw on his chest, pressing tight. Then I took a step back and turned away from him, trying to show him that I meant him no harm but that I was higher up on the chain. He pulled on my tail and I snapped my neck back, showing him my long, sharp teeth. I growled deeply but didn't attack.

Stop.

I was the fucking Fated Alpha; I wouldn't be baited into a fight. I didn't believe that Shayne would actually try to kill me.

The image of my dad, hands deep into a clock, trying to fit a complicated piece into the right place came to my mind. Shayne picked me up and placed me on the desk.

Jumping up, Shayne leaped onto my back, tearing into its length. I yelped as his claws ripped into my hind quarter and pain shot up my backside. A glance at it showed my red muscles protruding through the fur.

Did you think that just because you can shift now, that you could tell me what to do? That because you were once the Fated Alpha, that you are my Alpha now?

Growling, I nipped at his muzzle then jumped backwards, out of the reach of his teeth. The pain moved down my legs and I licked at the wound. He tried to jump on me again but I shot forward, the saliva from my tongue already healing the wound in my back. He came after me again and this time I faced him head on.

Back the fuck up, Shayne. I know you don't want to do this.

You need to earn your place as my Alpha. You need to really mean it, that you will kill me if I don't acquiesce to your leadership.

Was he trying to tell me something?

Suddenly a dark grey wolf came into the fringe of my view. He leaped through the air and I braced for the impact. Instead of tackling me, he landed beyond me to tackle Shayne.

They rolled through the forest floor, banging and slipping through the trees. Their growls made a hell of a noise. They were a blur of fur and snapping bones. Their piss flew through the air, showering the trees and leaves.

Then the grey wolf clutched at Shayne's throat and threw his head back and forth.

I remembered Shayne cleaning off my knee and then reaching into his pocket, pulling out a chocolate wrapped in gold foil. He handed it over to me with a smile.

Rage rolled over my body at the attack on Shayne. It could only mean that he was going to take me hostage. Then Garrett would humiliate and torture me before the pack. It also meant that Shayne had been used as a pawn to draw me out.

Letting my rage roll over my body, I attacked.

I would kill him because Shayne was *mine*. And we always protect the pack.

I landed on the foreign wolf's back. My teeth ripped into his side and I jerked my head to tear into his fur, pulling him off of Shayne.

He yelped, letting go of Shayne's neck, who rolled back out of sight. The wolf turned now to defend himself and I jumped on top of him, aiming for his neck. I caught it in between my teeth. Gripping it tight, he turned and twisted his body, trying to throw me off. I moved with him, still hanging on until he used his paws to push me off him. I slid down his body, biting and clawing, trying to get a hold on him again.

Then he jerked back and jumped toward me. He tried to throw me on my back but I was too big for him. I met him with my own leap. My jaw met him right at the sensitive part of his throat. His neck went slack in my mouth and I crushed it as tight as my jaws would bite.

He fell onto his back, showing me his belly but I ignored his submission. I didn't trust him; he would kill me as soon as I turned my back. I stepped onto his belly and yanked my head back, snapping his neck. He hung, limp, in my teeth.

I felt a rush of power flow through my body and I snapped my head back and forth with his neck still in my mouth. When I was sure that he was dead, I dropped him and rushed towards Shayne, who was watching me with wide eyes.

I placed my head over his neck, wagging my tail. I meant him no harm but I was the dominant wolf between the two of us. He licked his lips, placing his head on my shoulder, agreeing to submit to me. He tried to slink off, still not completely submissive, so I stepped in his path. I barred his retreat with my head still over his neck.

I wasn't done with him yet.

He bent his head down, ears perked up and back legs stiff, still not quite acquiescing.

I growled and this time the sound of it echoed through the trees. *I don't need to kill you, but I will kill for you, to protect you.*

I showed my teeth and he stopped moving to allow me to move my head over his. Then he bowed his head low and I jumped up, my front legs pawing at his head. He slipped out from under me, trying to run off again.

Oh, hell no. He wasn't leaving without complete submission to me. I bit the top of his neck. It was hard enough to draw blood.

This time, he submitted. He laid down and showed me his stomach with his head and tail tucked close to the ground.

I stood over him. *You are mine now, Shayne. And you will be my spy for me.*

He whined.

You must. We cannot allow Garret to be Alpha over the pack. He will destroy it.

Shayne whined again but he pawed at my stomach softly. I knew that he would do it.

Good.

I backed away, allowing him to stand up. I bit his muzzle softly, chastising him, then licked it. He kept his head lower than mine and I continued to lick his muzzle until he gave me a lick. Then he nipped at my neck and I noticed for the first time that I was wearing the necklace my mom gave me.

You are never to tell anyone of this necklace.

He bowed again.

I realized I'd lost the other two necklaces but I didn't stop to worry about that now.

I looked up, still keeping my head over his to look out over the forest, feeling a little bit of shame for killing the other wolf. But I knew it had to be done. Light glowed from the south end of the forest and I realized that I'd taken too long to assert my dominance.

I need to go.

He whined and I licked him one last time, then I turned to run back towards the road. He followed behind me. Suddenly, my little kitten ran out of the trees to follow me with her short little legs. I slowed my pace just a little bit to allow her to keep up.

Guess I've got a new kitten. As soon as we reached the road, Shayne held back, not wanting to be seen by my pack. I let him stay, knowing it was the right thing to do even though I wished he could come with me. To have a little bit of my pack with me would be a comfort.

I began to jog, feeling the need to hurry and I threw my words at him as I followed the road towards the highway. *I'll be in touch.*

His farewell hit me like a ton of bricks. *You should know, Aaron is engaged to Olivia.*

I stumbled to the ground, unable to pick myself up as grief ripped through my chest. I looked back to ask him if Aaron had agreed to it of his own will, but Shayne was gone. My kitten came up to me slowly and began to lick the tears streaming down my muzzle, trying to comfort me. I laid down on the road, listening to the fighting coming from the woods but I couldn't get up.

How could he do that to me? He said he would find me. Did he just agree to it to placate his dad?

In that moment, I came to the realization that my hopes for Aaron and me were just a dream. I'd held onto it for so long, even as Aaron began to distance himself from me, not wanting to accept reality.

But Aaron accepted the truth long before I did.

Although Aaron said he would find me, he would have to leave his family to make that happen. Maybe that was was what he *wanted*, but I knew Aaron; he would never leave his family defenseless. And I didn't want him to; he had to protect them.

I put my nose on my paws and cried, feeling the song of death and grief pour out of me.

I lay there with my cat snuggled next to me for I don't know how long, until I heard the rumble of thunder above me. I looked up to a cloudless sky and realized that it wasn't thunder but the roar of dragon wings. They'd all shifted now and were circling high up, searching for me. The wind from their wings snuffed out the fires threatening to take over the woods and caused a whoosh of air to run over me.

My new pack.

I pushed myself up, willing myself to move and run towards the meeting point.

❧

ONLY AVERY WAS CLOSE ENOUGH TO THE ROAD, FLYING UP AND DOWN IT searching for me. I galloped towards him, howling to get his attention. As soon as he saw me, he rushed towards me, flying closer to the ground. Then he stretched his head down at me.

Awe.

I leaned up and rubbed my head against his. As soon as we moved to join the other dragons, two grey wolves barreled out of the woods and leaped in the air. I've never seen wolves fly so high or steady as they landed on top of him.

One of them caught on to Avery's wing, shredding it with his large claws. The other one, with spattered white on his face, landed on top of Avery. He bit into Avery's shoulder.

Avery careened through the air before landing and skidding across the asphalt road.

I raced to help him, leaping onto the white-faced wolf on his back. I scratched him with my long claws but he didn't let go. Avery swung his wings, trying to throw him off. The wolf flew through the air, shoving me.

I fell off and rolled on the ground, landing against a tree. Pain shot up my spine and I let out a yelp, paralyzed in my hind legs.

I sat, angry and immobile as I stared at the two wolves attacking Avery. Stupid freaking wolves and stupid freaking tree. What the hell. My back grew warm as a flow of magic ran down it. I knew that my body was trying to heal itself.

Avery hit one of them with his spiky tail, running deep gashes down the dark grey wolf's side. The bitter smell of his blood hit my nose. Even my little kitten entered the fray, hissing and batting at the wolves. I looked to the sky for help but the rest of the guys were still circling, looking for us. I tried to reach out to them mentally, but they were too far away.

Yipping impatiently at my wolf magic, I urged it to work faster. Warmth spread through my torso, then my feet and paws.

Suddenly my cat flew through the air and my stomach dropped. She tumbled to the ground, rolling. After a brief moment of staring into the woods, she stood up and relief flowed through my body. Those assholes had no right to attack the cutest cat this side of the Mississippi.

No way was I going to let them get away with that.

As soon as my body completely healed, I jumped up and attacked. The white-faced wolf had Avery on his back, still attempting to grip his throat, while the darker one was clawing at his wings. I jumped on top of the white-faced one, teeth bared and a warning growl in my throat. I pushed him off Avery and he lunged at me. We met in the air, paws up, claws out. His claws landed on my face, ripping through my eye. My blood dripped down my muzzle. The hair on the back of my neck stood on end as my rage reared its head.

I will kill this motherfucking wolf.

I flew at him in a frenzy, teeth gnashing, claws scraping. His teeth landed on my throat and I rolled to the ground, gripping him to me with my front feet. Using my back feet, I scraped against the soft underbelly and my claws sliced into his stomach.

He howled, letting go of my throat and yanking his head from in between my paws. He fell backwards, bleeding from his stomach.

Glancing over at Avery, he had the dark-haired wolf in between his sharp teeth and was crushing his neck. I landed on the white-faced wolf and clamped down on his neck. He pushed against me weakly but I held him tight and felt his blood gush down the bottom of my jaw and into my fur.

Finally his struggling softened until it stopped. I yanked my head back and forth for good measure.

Take that, asshole.

I dropped the wolf and, after making sure he was really dead, I ran back towards Avery. He was on top of the wolf and flapping his shredded wings in a victory dance. I watched as he moved gracefully over the wolf, mesmerized by his elegance. Small streaks of fire spit from his mouth, sizzling the edges of the wolf's fur.

I turned back towards the woods, sensing the awareness of other wolves. His fire dance was sparking their attention.

Avery. We need to go.

I felt his adrenaline as he stomped on the wolf with his clawed feet.

Avery. I ran to pick up my kitten; she was curled up on the ground sleeping. I yanked the back of her neck with my teeth and ran towards Avery, plowing into him. We tumbled to the ground and, for a moment, I thought he was going to snap at me with his sharp teeth. Instead he shook his head, coming to.

We need to get out of here or more wolves will be here soon.

As I struggled to disentangle myself from him, he rolled to the side to help me. As soon as I leapt off him, careful not to hurt him with my claws, he dragged himself onto his feet.

For a moment he was motionless as he rose in the air. Then he dove sharply, almost crashing to the ground. He landed harshly, rolling over the asphalt and giving himself road rash.

I ran back to him, feeling horrible. His wings were beginning to heal but there were a few large tears still in them. I remembered how Aaron used to lick my wounds and I wondered if that would actually work.

I placed the cat on the ground and, stretching my neck, worked my tongue softly over his wings. He stepped closer, maneuvering them to help me and I saw that it was working. The soft tissue of his wings molded together and when I was done, he stepped back, testing them. A soft wave of wind rushed over my body and caused the hair on my back to stand up. He moved higher into the air and, after picking up the kitten again, I began to run.

Glancing up, I could see that Avery had risen high into the air. He breathed a blaze of fire so the other dragons could see it. They flew towards us and I ran faster, feeling a rush of pleasure as my body moved soundlessly over the pavement.

The dragons were behind me for a brief moment and I felt a wave of air as they circled over me. Then they moved onward and only the blue-scaled dragon stayed with me as I raced down the road towards the runway.

₨

IT TOOK ME A WHILE TO SHIFT BACK INTO MY HUMAN FORM AND AVERY waited for me patiently, then we walked into the spotlights of the private bay at the small airport. The copilot didn't even blink an eye at our naked bodies or the cat who walked up the stairs with me. He held out blankets as we climbed up the stairs and I wrapped myself up in its softness, giving him a grateful nod.

He nodded back at me. "We have permission to leave in about thirty minutes."

As soon as we were inside, he closed the door and moved towards the front where the pilot was running the engine.

Easton was already dressed and sitting in a large leather chair, staring out the window with a scowl on his face. I looked out the window, making sure that the pack hadn't caught up with us. What if we didn't make it out before they came for us?

Christian was pulling his shirt over his body and I glimpsed at his perfectly sculpted abs before they disappeared under his shirt. Avery was rummaging through a cabinet, pulling out a pair of jeans and grumbling to himself.

I looked around, trying to find something I could wear and was tempted to just fall into the seat naked. I was exhausted. Hunter stepped up to me; he was dressed in jeans and a black t-shirt and in his hands was another pair of clothes.

He frowned, staring at me intently. "These may be a bit big but we didn't have the chance to put any extra clothes for you on the plane."

I nodded and put my hand on them. "It's okay, I understand." I tried to take the clothes from him, but he wouldn't let them go. He gave me a dark look, his eyes staring into mine intently.

Did I do something to him? I could understand Easton and Avery; they were always grumpy but not Hunter. After a moment, he released his hold on the clothes and then he slumped into the chair next to where I stood.

I tried to get dressed under the blanket but it was difficult. Hunter respectfully averted his eyes, though I caught him trying to catch a glimpse before his eyes became glued to the front of the plane.

Avery was complaining to his skinny jeans as he struggled to get them on and I wanted to laugh at him. Instead, I held onto the blanket with one hand while trying to slip some blue boxer briefs on, hoping that they were clean. Christian moved to stand next to me and his hands folded over mine as they gripped the blanket. I stared into his gaze briefly as I slipped my hands out from under his to try to wrangle the underwear on. As soon as I was dressed, though braless, he folded the blanket and sat next to Easton.

Sadness clung to me. I'd left behind the gun, the only possession I owned from my parents and I wanted to cry. I'd also left behind Carrie and Aaron's necklace; they busted from me when I shifted. The symbolism of my whole life with Aaron and my family left behind wasn't lost on me. I bit my lip, holding in my tears. There would be time for that later, when I was alone.

Finally getting his pants on, Avery collapsed, shirtless, into the chair across from me and stretched his legs out onto Easton's lap. Easton turned his lip up and brushed them off. Avery moved his legs onto Christian's knees who just placed his hands over Avery's bare feet.

Easton sat up in his chair, his back as straight as a board.

"Here it comes." Avery folded his hands behind his head and tried to relax but I could see lines of tension in his body.

"What the hell happened back there?" Easton turned to stare at each of us and a blush crept onto my face when he looked at me. I had no idea what he was talking about.

Christian answered first; he was massaging Avery's feet whose face was scrunched up like the massage was hurting him. "Which part, Easton?"

Easton eyed me, staring a hole into my chest. "Did any of you know she had the necklace?" My hand went to it. I guess they'd all seen it now.

Both Christian and Avery shook their heads but Hunter didn't move; he just stared out the window with an angry scowl on his face.

"If I would've known that she had the necklace, I wouldn't let her shift in front of all of us. Not all of us at the same time."

Hunter finally spoke. "We were trying to keep her from burning alive."

"If she hadn't gone for that cat, she would've been okay. We would've made it out through the window."

Something heckled inside of me. "Are you saying I shouldn't have saved the kitten?" She was curled up in my lap right now and my fingers moved over her.

"Of course not. But you shouldn't have had a cat in the first place, not when our lives were on the line. You or the cat could've died."

I felt my throat go dry. He was right, of course.

Hunter turned to face him. "Why does it matter? What's done is done."

Easton frowned. "It may not matter to you, but it matters to me. None of us planned on that happening."

"What happened?" I couldn't hold back. "I have no idea what you're talking about. How did you know about the necklace?"

Hunter took my hand and squeezed it too tight. "Elizabeth had no idea that was going to happen but her mother gave her the necklace for a reason. Jane knew that this birthday was going to be risky. Why give it to Elizabeth if she didn't intend for her to use it?"

I yanked my hand out of his. "Quit talking about me as if I'm not here."

Christian pushed Avery's feet off of his lap and leaned forward. "Don't take it personally, Elizabeth. They're just frustrated, is all. No one knew that the necklace would react the way it did."

Anger rolled in my stomach and it made me feel sick. "But what did the necklace do? Will someone please tell me?"

The plane grew silent and the only sounds were of the pilots talking to each other in the cockpit. Only Christian looked at me, a guilty look on his face but he didn't explain.

I stood up abruptly; the kitten jumped to the floor with a hiss and ran under Christian's seat. "Since none of you will tell me, I'll just leave."

Christian held his hand up. "Elizabeth."

"It's okay. I need to go to the bathroom anyway."

No one tried to stop me and I went towards the back of the plane, hoping there actually was a bathroom back here. Footsteps followed behind me but I didn't turn to see who it was.

As soon as I closed the bathroom door, there was a firm knock on it. I opened it to peek out and Hunter threw the door back, rushed inside and then slammed it shut behind him.

I jumped out of his way. "Did I do something to you to make you angry with me?"

His large frame filled the bathroom and I pressed against the back of the sink to make room for him. He put his hands on the counter, blocking me in. His eyes stared deeply into mine, as if he was searching for something.

I held my breath, waiting for him to tell me why he followed me in here, yet still hoping he would do something more. That he would fill the space inside of me that was hurting and empty. I felt so warm every time he was near; my body responded in a way it had never responded before and I wanted him to press against me closer. Instead he tugged on a strand of my hair.

He took in a deep breath. "It took you so long to come out of the woods…"

He paused and I wondered if he expected me to answer him. To explain what took me so long. I blinked, trying to come up with an answer.

Instead, he continued. "I thought that your tracker killed you, or that you were killed by your pack. I didn't know what happened and I was circling the woods, afraid that I would find your dead body." He squeezed his eyes closed for a second and when he opened them back up, his stare was so fierce, I couldn't move.

"And it felt like something broke me."

I was speechless, shocked by the force of his words. Like he cared about this silly little girl he just met.

"You just met me." It was all I could think of to say.

He shook his head and I swallowed hard, feeling the intensity of his passion as it washed over me. "No. I've been dreaming about you for five years. I knew from the minute I saw you in that car that you were the woman of my dreams."

MY EYEBROWS FLEW UP. "YOU'VE DREAMED ABOUT ME?"

Hunter nodded and grasped my jaw, pulling me close. "You are my mate, Elizabeth. You're going to change my life forever."

I tried to pull my head back, to draw myself out of the intensity of his feelings but he gripped me harder, forcing me to stare into his eyes.

How could I change anything about his life?

"You just came to rescue me. I appreciate everything that you've done but I have to get back to my pack. They need me." I almost said that I already had a mate but the sentence caught in my throat. Aaron was mine no longer; he'd taken another. Even if he was forced to do it. The thought burned my stomach.

Hunter's other hand moved around my back and he pulled me closer; he was clinging to me like a lifeline. "We need you."

"What does that mean?"

"We've been training together for five years and yet not one of us has emerged as the Alpha."

"I thought that Avery... Christian, they look up to you. Avery called you the boss."

"And yet Easton, he refuses to submit to me. I can only be Alpha if the whole pack supports me."

"Easton will never submit to me."

He nodded. "He will. He already has, he just doesn't know it yet." His eyes bore into mine and I felt his heart pounding against my chest, we were that tightly entwined.

"I can't be your Alpha. I have to save my pack from Garrett; he'll destroy the pack if I don't save them."

"And yet, you bound yourself to us."

"What does that mean?"

"When you shifted, you marked us as yours. You staked a claim on us, as a potential mate."

I swallowed hard. "A claim on *all* of you?"

Even though he nodded, answering me, he didn't need to because as soon as the words left my mouth, I knew the truth. The magic of the necklace had read the deep desires of my heart, so deep that I hadn't even realized it yet.

That I felt a strange and profound desire to be with them. That I wasn't supposed to be alpha over one of the biggest packs in the southeastern United States but of something much greater, more *majestic* than that.

The wolf inside me purred, knowing that this was *meant* to happen.

Still nodding, his fingers pressed into my back. "For years, your face has haunted my sleep. Taunting and teasing me, I thought I would never meet you. And then, I saw you in that car and I... I'd seen it before. I knew it was you. And I knew I had to save you, to be with you."

He looked away. "I hoped that you'd feel the same way, that maybe you'd had the same dreams but..." His voice faded as he stared over my shoulder. "Easton thinks that my dreams may be part of my shifter magic. So I wasn't too surprised that you'd never dreamed of me. Which was..." He looked back at me and I could hear him swallow hard. "...so disappointing."

His eyes studied mine for a while. I was shocked at his words yet I couldn't deny how I'd felt when I saw him for the first time. The feeling that he was meant to be in my life, that my life was meant for something more. And yet, my own heart was still torn between him and Aaron.

I pressed my hands to his chest and stared up into his eyes, wishing that he would explain what the hell was going on. When I didn't answer, he continued.

"When I couldn't find you in the woods tonight; I thought you were dead and in those moments, I thought I would die. I'd finally met my mate and had lost her so quickly."

And suddenly, my body was responding to him; my heart was pounding so hard that I thought it would burst, accidentally falling out of my chest and tumbling to the floor. His azure blue eyes stared into my soul as if they could see my every secret. His body, pressing against mine, revealed the cut of his muscles and the small dip in his stomach. I wanted to run my hands over it, to cup his face in my hands and kiss away his worries. The magic of my wolf ran through my body, ready to claim what was offered.

"Answer me, Princess. I need to know what you think." I felt his emotion coming off him in waves and I reveled in the feeling of his adoration. But I didn't know how to answer. How to tell him that he was the most beautiful warrior I'd ever seen. That he exuded power like the soldiers of old who knew how to fight for what they wanted. That from the very moment he'd wrapped his legs around mine in the woods, that my body and soul knew that he was *mine*.

"I— Hunter, I..." I swallowed hard then took his hand and nipped his fingertips roughly.

His other hand moved to the back of my neck, pulling my mouth so close to his that his lips moved against mine. "Tell me, Princess. Say it."

I closed my eyes, putting my hands to his face and the desire to claim him for myself poured over me, living and pulsing inside of me. My wolf emerged, steady and sure; she knew what she wanted. And she wasn't afraid to claim it. I unleashed her power, trusting her. I growled. "Yes, Hunter. You are fucking *mine*."

That was all it took and then his mouth closed over mine, devouring me like a drowning man would take his first breath of air. His thumbs pressed into my cheeks and I wrapped my legs around his back, pulling him in closer.

He pulled back and his eyes stared into mine. "I've waited so long for this moment. From here on out, your body and soul will be mine."

All my anger and fear moved through my body, pulsing and fierce, and the need to feel something else was all-consuming. Something else besides grief for the loss of my parents, for the loss of my life as I knew it. The need to feel *him* in my arms, someone who could protect not only my body but my heart.

I threw my arms around his neck, pressing him close as my mouth opened, kissing him passionately. His mouth claimed mine, moving against it possessively. His hands were grasping my jaw as his tongue explored my mouth and I reveled in the sensation that ran through my body. I was pressed back against the mirror but I pulled him closer, trapping his body against mine. I felt his fire and his fervor, demanding me to bind myself to him and I matched it with my own need.

I needed him to be mine.

He said that I'd marked him, that I'd marked all of them.

Power enveloped my body as blue sparks flew from my necklace and I poured all of my energy and passion into it, making it pulse through our bodies. It wrapped around us, as it had in the cabin, binding him to me. It was the same force that had marked them to me, *all* of them at once; the unknown desire of my heart and the fate of the moon that brought them to me.

I knew in that moment that I would do everything in my power to protect them. I felt a growl deep in my throat as a possessiveness washed over me; he was mine. *They* were mine, *all* of them.

❧

THEN THE PLANE JERKED FORWARD, PREPARING TO LEAVE AND I GASPED, surprised. Hunter's mouth twisted into a grin but he kissed me again, softer now until he pulled back.

I raised my eyebrows. "I guess we should get seated."

He pressed my hand to the space over his chest where his heart was, staring into my eyes. His look, raw and passionate, broke something inside of me and a tear tracked down my face.

He wiped at it but I held the rest inside, the instinct to never show weakness so ingrained in my soul that even now, when it was just Hunter and me, I had to hide it.

He kissed my forehead and I raised myself up to kiss him softly on the lips. He pulled the back of my head towards him, sealing his lips over mine, kissing me deeply. Then he pulled back and I forced a smile, trying not to let any more tears flow.

He opened the door and held my hand as we made our way down the short hallway. The plane was gathering speed over the runway and we needed to get seated.

The other guys immediately saw that we were holding hands but Hunter ignored their strange looks. I looked at the floor, unwilling to look them in the eyes as we made our way towards our seats. I sensed some anger around me but I wasn't sure I wanted to know why.

Then something hit the window next to where I was standing. I jumped and turned towards the window. My mouth dropped open as

I peered through it: the outer window was shattered and the inner window had large cracks through it. It wouldn't take much for it to fall out.

Sprinting down the runway with us was a newly shifted golden-red wolf, his clothes strewn out on the ground, along with several other grey and golden wolves. I froze in shock, staring at Garrett as he tried to keep up with the plane.

Hunter pressed beside me, and then Easton was there.

"The window's destroyed."

The co-pilot rushed from the cockpit. "What happened? We have a warning that pressure is leaking from the plane."

Easton pointed to the window. "We need to stop the plane. We can't fly like that."

The co-pilot's eyes widened. "I'll let the pilot know immediately."

Hunter grabbed the co-pilot's arm and pointed out the window. "If you stop this plane, we'll all be killed." There were hundreds of wolves now racing towards us; we had no chance of survival if we stayed.

The co-pilot pressed his face to a window.

Hunter let go of his arm. "Can you fly this plane out of here? To the nearest airport, just to get us to a safe place?"

"Are you crazy?" Easton tried pushing the co-pilot towards the front, who wasn't budging. "He can't fly like this. It'll create a vacuum and spit us all out. Go tell the pilot to stop."

The co-pilot turned to look at Avery and Christian who were on the edge of their seats. Avery had his hands on the buckle of his jeans, ready for action if he needed to shift.

"Actually we can. If we fly low enough. It just may be possible." The co-pilot began to move towards the front of the plane. "Everyone buckle up. As tight as you can."

"It may be possible? I'd rather take my chances with them." Easton pointed his thumb at the window.

The co-pilot turned on his heel, giving Easton a sharp look. "You may be willing but I'm not. Sit down and hang on tight." He moved back towards the cockpit, calling over his shoulder. "And use the oxygen masks if you need them."

"Shit." Easton hit the side of the plane, his face red.

I put my hand on his shoulder. "We'll be okay, I'm sure the pilots know what they're doing."

Hunter pushed me into my seat. "Easton, just shut the fuck up and strap yourself in." Avery was sitting back into his seat now, pulling his seatbelt tight. I grabbed mine and clasped it so tight it hurt my stomach.

Grumbling, Easton buckled himself him and I noticed that Christian was buckled tight and closing his eyes, breathing deeply. My nails dug into my seatbelt, angry at Garrett for risking their lives again to try to get at me.

Then we flew down the runway and the sound of the wheels on the tarmac roared in my wolf ears. Impulsively, I unbuckled myself and ran to another window. Ignoring the cries of the guys, I made out Garret's wolf-form on the runway. I stared at him, allowing my anger to flow through my veins and my Alpha power to pulse through my body. And in that moment, I made a promise.

I *will* challenge him one day. I *will* avenge the death of my parents and take my rightful place as Alpha of the Southeastern White Tooth Pack. And I will *enjoy* it as I feel the last of his pulse between my teeth as he dies at my hand.

I grinned as I told myself that Aaron was right. There is more to leading a pack besides just being a wolf, and Garret was going to find out just how well I could play the game. The plane left the ground and I gave Garrett the bird.

Suddenly, Hunter's strong arms surrounded me, pulling me from the window and the sound of voices filled my ears.

"Elizabeth, sit down!"

"You're going to get hurt!"

I turned to Hunter, anger flushing my face, and he firmly placed me in the cool leather chair.

"Sit down, Elizabeth."

I growled but buckled my seat belt as Hunter sat beside me. The plane shifted as it gained altitude and I turned to look at Easton.

He held a tight frown and gripped the arms of his seat. I braced myself, waiting for him to yell at me for being so careless, for putting Hunter at risk.

Instead, his words surprised me.

"I hate flying." He stared at me for only a moment longer before looking away.

Then there was a large popping noise and the inner window flew across the plane. It whipped by my face, barely missing me, and crashed against the window facing it. The other window broke, creating a roaring flow of air through the cabin and the plane dropped a few feet. I gripped Hunter's arm, staring into his widened eyes as fear struck my heart. "Oh shit."

PLEASE

Note from the Author:

I would love it if you wrote a review. It would make my heart beat so hard that it might explode!!!

Thank you!

65646964R00068

Made in the USA
Middletown, DE
02 March 2018